Madams Wear Black

by

Gregory Montoya

Last Laugh Productions
Walnut Creek, CA

Cover art by Bing Image Creator

www.lastlaughproductions.org

Logo by Bradley Stockwell

Breakage

This was a poem about a flower. That didn't
work — *now it's a poem about a broken pot.*
                    — *James Norman*

All my poems, songs and stories
start with the broken pot
Nothing much happened till I shattered

The seed cannot grow till it breaks open
the plum can't be tasted without
tearing the skin

My story is about tasting something bitter,
spitting it out
burying it
and crying

Tears are water
In time comes a tree
and even
someone to tend it

Such perfect fruit!

— Deborah Fruchey, from *Hint*
(Last Laugh Productions, 2024)

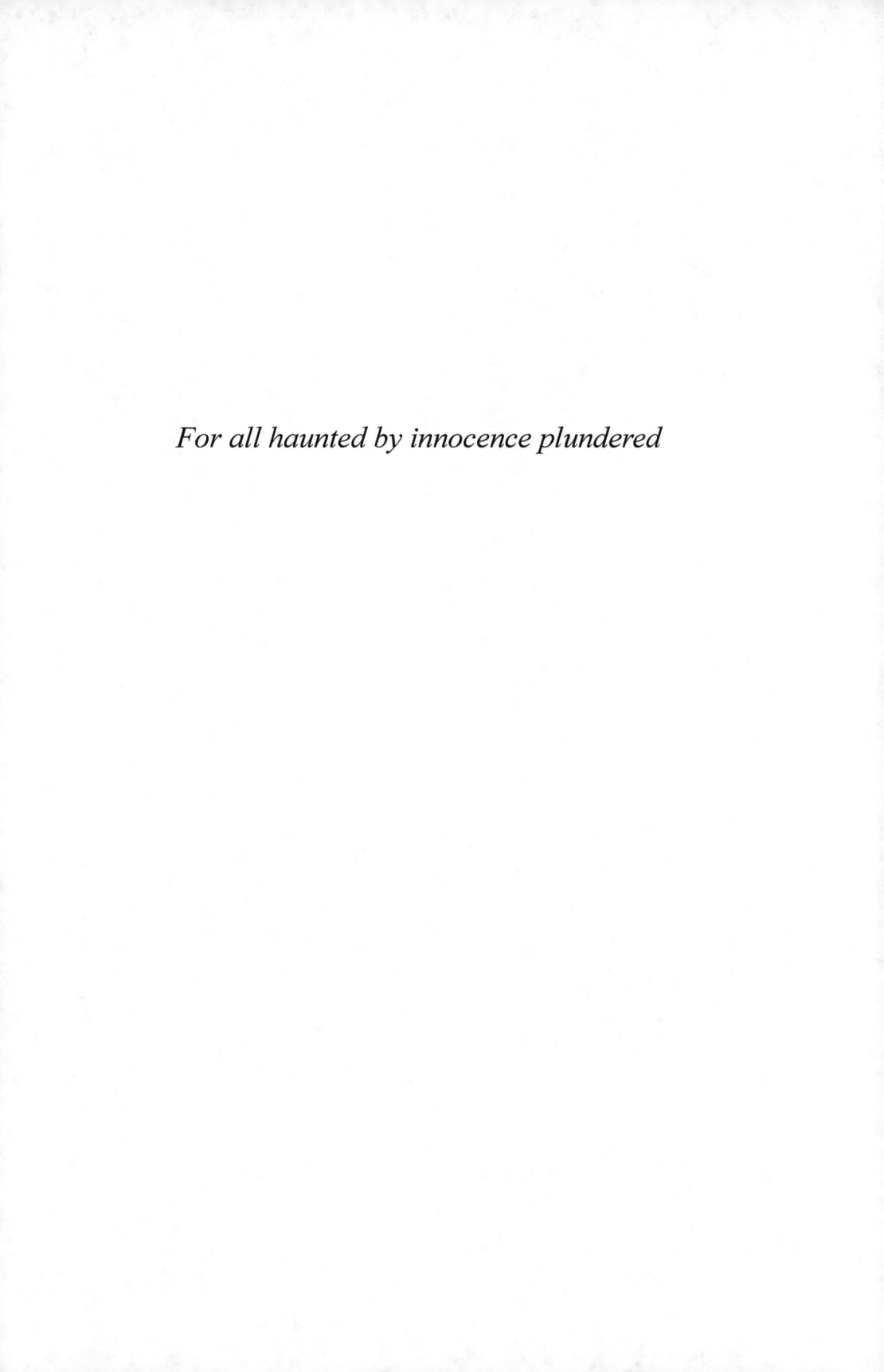

For all haunted by innocence plundered

Table of Contents

ONE

I lay naked, face down upon the floor mattress, as she set the Styrofoam cup of tea near my pillow. Its bloated tea bag blistered the surface. Every illicit massage parlor I'd visited offered tea. And I'd be damned if it didn't always arrive without sugar or honey. I never declined the offer, though I didn't drink the stuff either. It was the predictability that warmed me. I chuckled at the steamy custom.

My "masseuse" slipped off her stilettos, knelt down beside me, and let her thigh press against mine. My breath humidified. I snuggled my cheek into the pillow and noted that healers always displayed an external statement of purpose. A clerical collar, scrubs, or a body glove miniskirt like hers.

She bent forward to bring her lips to my ear. "What's your name?" Her faint accent might've been Thai, Vietnamese, or even Lao. But it was too slight to tell. Made me think she'd been in the US for some time. She'd also bleached her hair blonde. Another tip that she'd been here a while. And I'd chosen her for her sexy, age-defying maturity.

"Cisco," I lied. "And yours?"

"Jasmine. How do you like massage? Hard, medium, or soft?"

"Soft," I answered as if it mattered, and anticipated the next bump in the way of her touch. It didn't take long. Her gentle fingers hesitated upon my first twisted scar.

"Burns, alright? They don't hurt." I hadn't meant to sound harsh.

Silently, she resumed her kneading, rapidly at first, skipping over the rest of my back's coarse blotches. She slowed her pace at my butt, where the terrain became peaceful again.

I turned on my back. "Sorry. Didn't mean to snap at you."

"How 'sorry' are you?" she replied and began gently stroking Mr. Happy to inflate both me and the price of my redemption—a disadvantage I breathlessly didn't resist.

I got up to empty my wallet without a dip in my rigid anticipation. I returned with my penance and reclined upon the mattress.

Jasmine plucked the cash from my fingertips. "I'll be right back." She padded out of the room in her bare feet.

Though accustomed to working girls' practice of stashing their cash before granting quarter, the break always strained into an eternity.

Finally, a soft knock at the door announced her return. With her smile aimed directly at me, she unbuttoned her blouse and dropped it to the floor. Her lacy bra and thong followed.

Braced up on my elbow, I watched as she peeled off her skirt.

Jasmine crouched, reached under the mattress to pull out a condom, and then tapped my chest. "Lay back, honey."

She tore open the wrapper and tucked the rubber behind her grin. Then she guided Mr. Happy into her mouth, delicately unrolling the condom from between her teeth as she swallowed me.

Her tenderly bobbing and swiveling head stirred my body into a caldron of passion. I gently ran my fingers through her hair.

Craving more than her slathering tongue, I gasped, "Can we fuck?"

Jasmine kissed Mr. Happy's head and then straddled me like a cowgirl. She reached down and slipped me into her moist delta. Harmonics that had nothing to do with sound cascaded throughout my body.

All my hunger for a woman's embrace swooped up inside her, igniting a fusillade of delight. I thrust for unachievable depth as my fingers massaged her abundant ass.

I rose up and kissed her natural breasts and then drew her down as I reclined again. Swimming in each other's arms, I rolled us over. Beneath me, her breasts pressed against mine. Jasmine's hips rhythmically matched Mr. Happy's hungry strokes until I exploded out of my solitude. A moan rumbled from my throat. I fell limp upon her, spent and panting.

She tapped my shoulder and whispered, "You're heavy. Hard to breathe."

I slid off next to her, pacified at the end of our transaction. Safe that we'd touched each other but kept our hearts out of reach. "Thank you," I said, my gratitude sincere. She'd never bleed like others I'd loved. Only my best friend Margo had been smart enough to stop at friendship.

Jasmine excused herself, and I dipped my chin. I knew the drill. She'd return with a warm, wet washcloth and wipe down Mr. Happy. Then, after we dressed, she'd walk me to the door, hug me, or even kiss me goodbye. Beyond "happy endings," I'd found sanctuary in illicit massage parlors' predictable charm.

Pillowing the back of my head in my palms, I gazed up at the exposed HVAC ducts and decided I'd come back for Jasmine the next time Mr. Happy demanded succor. If she stuck around. But these girls were as fickle as me and didn't stay in one place long. Can't get attached if you keep moving.

I flicked my Zippo, strolling to my car. It had been with me since Vietnam. Sometimes, I didn't know I was playing with it until its clicks penetrated my ears. I'd bought it after witnessing my first napalm strike. Then, I'd paid a Vietnamese engraver to inscribe the lighter with *Napalm sticks to kids too,* so I'd never forget what I'd seen. By the time I caught on that those images were as seared into my brain as those words were chiseled into steel, I couldn't let go of the damn thing. The click of its precision spring and the touch of its polished edges somehow relaxed me.

Margo, a psychologist, called it my talisman. Told me that my Zippo's harmless clicks spoke to my true nature. Not that scared kid's terrorized into unleashing his rifle's deadly bark. *Psychobabble*, I'd countered.

Click, click. Click, click. Time to head to my dad's house. I switched on my pager to see a number I didn't recognize. I found a pay phone and dialed the number: "White Memorial Hospital, how may I direct your call?"

Pop had died by the time I reached the ER. Waist bent, I stretched my arms against the counter, my head suspended between my elbows.

"I'm sorry, Mr. Soze. Would you like to see a chaplain?"

I stood to face the nurse. "No. I have to see my father."

"He's no longer in the emergency room. You'll be able to see him after he's transferred to the mortuary."

It'd been a week since I'd seen him, but he'd called me last night. Demanded to know if I'd lost his address and phone number? Damned my *I'm busy at work* excuse. I couldn't tell him that it sickened me to watch cancer eat him alive, so I'd gotten testy with the old mechanic. *I'm a CPA, not freed at five by the punch of a time clock*, I'd said. He'd slugged back with his usual jab, *When are you gonna knock that chip off your shoulder?* I'd sucked up his familiar accusation and told him I'd visit him today.

"I promised to see him today," and read her recoiling squint as 'You don't get it? You're too late.'

A pink cancer ribbon covered her last name on her ID badge, but Jane found herself at the wrong end of my rifled glare. "You don't understand....*Jane*. The only way I'm leaving here without seeing him is handcuffed in the back of a cop car."

Jane stared at me while she backed through the door at the rear of the nurses' station.

A moment later I heard, "Ahem." I turned into the leer of a young hospital rent-a-cop. He stood with his feet apart, his thumbs hooked into his utility belt. Twenty years ago, in 1969, the sight of Vietcong half his size clamped my ass. Not him. I huffed in contempt.

The kid puffed his chest with a hiss and drew his hands to his sides. His fingers scratched the air.

A door whined open. Into the hall strutted a tall RN. Her taut gaze said she ran the place, not me. Jane followed in rapid half steps. A few feet away, she slowed, studying me. Jane bumped into her, but her boss didn't flinch.

My eyes caught the yellow and red striped Vietnam Service pin tacked to her Nurse Manager ID badge. Another determined African-American nurse burst out of my memory toward our burning chopper to drag me and the other wounded to safety. I blinked away the cruel images and, with them, scattered my resolve. I shook my head. "Please, ma'am. Let me say goodbye to my pop."

Her face relaxed. "This may not be the best time to see him," she said without judgment.

I focused on her war ribbon as if there I'd find the words to tell her we'd both seen worse.

Her eyes followed mine, and before I could speak, she asked, "Where?"

Taken aback, I heard myself say, "Mekong Delta."

She glanced at the security guard. "It's alright." Then, she turned to Jane. "Get an orderly."

"What?" Jane squeaked.

"You heard me," she said and turned to the miffed guard. "You heard me, too. It's alright."

Her voice softened. "Mr. Soze, an orderly will take you to see to your father."

My chin fell as I murmured, "I should've been here when he was still alive."

She reached up and squeezed my shoulder. "Your father never regained consciousness after the stroke that brought him here."

I bobbed my head. "I see. Thank you."

Following the orderly into the elevator, I battled a needling resentment that Pop had split before I...could apologize? I raked my face with my fingers but couldn't scrape away the guilty sting. Pop hadn't died to spite me. How fucked to think that? I reached for my Zippo.

My lighter's clicks drew no more than the orderly's side glance before we stepped into the basement's deserted hallway.

At the morgue he pushed open its double doors and flipped a switch. Fluorescent tubes sputtered on, emitting an irritable buzz that canceled my lighter's metallic clicks. I dropped it into my pocket.

Glancing between his three by five card and the labeled drawers of the morgue's refrigerator, the orderly sidestepped in search of Pop.

"Here it is," he announced as if he'd found his pen. He grimaced, then turned to me. "Your dad is right here."

He yanked on the lever and leaned back, allowing his weight to drag open the heavy drawer. The sight of the body bag spun me back to Nam again and sucked the wind out of me. I gulped air and watched the orderly draw down the zipper.

I caught my breath and helped him peel back the cold, crackling plastic before he stepped a polite distance away.

My gaze fell upon Pop's ashen face. Cancer had not been kind to the once robust mechanic. He lay shriveled and bent. Made me think that having to raise me alone had something to do with that.

Shame swelled inside of me. I wouldn't've turned off my pager if I'd kept my pants on. I could've been at Pop's side while his heart still beat. I leaned over and hugged his frigid chest. "Forgive me," I whispered.

I slowly withdrew and searched for the things I should've said. Then, I felt my fingernails gouging into my shoulders. I'd unconsciously crossed my arms. My jaw clenched against words Pop would never hear.

Pop told me not to mourn when he'd become terminal. He'd insisted life had been generous. That despite losing Mom, she'd left him with a fine son. I'd told him I wasn't sure about that, but he'd made me promise him a celebratory send-off.

I packed my lungs with breath and committed to making good on that promise. But my pledge hadn't relaxed my muscles. My lungs let go through a hiss, interrupting the orderly's exploration of a cracked tile with the toe of his shoe. He looked up.

"I could use some time alone. Mind if I find my own way out?"

"Of course not," he said and stepped toward Pop's extended drawer.

I hurried my stride to escape the zip of Pop's body bag.

Sealed alone in an elevator, I recalled Pop's demand to know if I'd lost his address and phone number? I leaned into the wall, my forehead braced upon my forearm. Memories screamed about my skull of the times I'd ducked under *I'm a busy CPA* to skip seeing him sick.

I cocked my fist to batter the wall, but Pop's complaint about *that chip* on my shoulder resounded between my ears. I splayed my fingers. Had he been right about me? I went for my

Zippo, but its sharp clicks dulled against my grief. I reached back against twenty years of trying to forget Vietnam and grabbed the club we used to beat back the war's misery. Under my breath, I repeated Nam's numbing mantra, "It don't mean nothin'," and pushed the first-floor button.

The doors opened at the lobby to a swarm of sad-eyed visitors. I squirmed through the crowd, barely feeling their bodies glance off mine. I headed for the parking lot.

Flopping into my sedan, I squeezed the wheel and tried concentrating on Pop's celebratory send-off.

Driving through Boyle Heights' familiar streets, I passed Evergreen Cemetery, and then by the barbershop where Pop used to take me when I was a kid. Smiley, the barber, kept a tame iguana in a huge fish tank. None of the gruff, blue-collar men who joked in their mixture of Spanish and English were as fascinated as I was by that laid-back lizard sunning itself in the shop window. What was that beast's name?—*Cucuy!* That was it. Smiley had said that he called the lizard bogeyman because it scared the pants off the neighborhood kids. I grinned at that sweet memory until it cramped my belly.

Sitting in my apartment under a single desk lamp, I stared at what I'd jotted down on my legal pad. I'd foolishly hoped that penciling out the details of Pop's goodbye would distract me from my kinked gut. But its spikes wouldn't let me ignore that hiding from heartache behind my CPA or in the cloisters of commercial sex had backfired.

I tossed down my pencil, stroked my stomach, and longed for my pal Margo's soothing voice. I started to reach for the phone but hesitated. She'd hop a plane to LAX if I told her Pop died. I couldn't impose. I'd wait until after his funeral.

Two

The company's board of directors had decided that a headquarters change of address to San Francisco would increase the firm's prestige, provide a viable real estate investment, and jettison older, high-paid staff who'd resign to stay in LA. Our NorCal branch operated out of a stately Market Street high-rise. The firm submitted an offer on the building.

My CFO boss called me into his office two weeks after I'd buried Pop. Asked me to take his place and fly to Frisco first thing in the morning with the Procurement VP. The sellers had made an acceptable counteroffer. He trusted my math and needed me to review the numbers before the VP signed. He also knew I'd no problem hopping a plane on short notice. Besides, the overnight trip would get me away from LA's gnashing reminders of Pop, and I'd get to see Margo.

In a drizzling Frisco, cooped up in a cab with the VP who bitched nonstop about having to uproot his family, I welcomed the business day's end. Back at our hotel, surrounded by the hotel district's baronial facades, I peered at the scattered clouds. The afternoon's sprinkles had dissipated with them.

The VP politely invited me to join him for dinner but offered little resistance to my decline. I'd employ room service to eat in peace before meeting Margo for drinks.

Showered and in a fresh suit, I hailed a cab and hoped it wasn't chauffeured by a chatty driver. I wanted to quietly indulge my muse—my longed-for rendezvous with Margo.

I slid into the back seat and asked the driver if he knew the Sunset Lounge? Me and Margo's favorite place to meet. With its unobstructed view of the Pacific, the crowded bar sat off the Great Highway. It served as a magnet for tourists and locals alike. I enjoyed the hive's anonymity.

"Great Highway," he said, giving me a two-finger salute before dropping the cab into gear.

I cracked the window. Inhaling the damp air, I stared outside and recalled the first time I saw my reflection in Margo's emerald eyes. In late 1970, I'd been home from Vietnam less than a year and felt surrounded by long-haired aliens—hippies.

A relentless sun-baked UCLA's quad as we undergrads stood in tedious registration lines. No sweat for me, though. LA's dry heat couldn't provoke glands calloused by Nam's jungle sauna. I considered my arid stand a booby prize.

A rogue breeze snatched one of my registration cards, whirling it to the ground behind me. I twisted in pursuit and tapped heads with a pretty coed. She'd also stooped to snag my wayward card. The tips of her fingers pressed my fluttering form to the cement while she scanned my face.

Intimidated by her beauty yet dazzled by the contrast of her green eyes against her cocoa complexion, I stood up empty-handed. "Excuse me—sorry."

"No harm done." Her long fingers draped her rich black hair over her shoulder in a fluid motion. She glanced down at my card. "Latin? Is that your major?" She stood up and held out the card.

"Ah...no. An elective. Accounting's my thing." I grasped for my card, but locked in her gaze, I missed. My arm fell. I reached out again but dodged her eyes.

She cupped my hand and pressed the card into my palm with her other hand. She waited until I mustered the strength to clasp it before her slender fingers slid away. I savored her velvet touch.

"So, how long have you been back?"

Her tapered waist divided a petite frame that stood well below my sinewy six feet. Yet she held the high ground. "Wha—what?"

"Vietnam. How long have you been back from the war?"

"What makes you think—"

"My brother Bobby came home in June. I know that haircut."

I stumbled back. "Guess I should let it grow."

"Up to you, *mijo.*" She extended her hand. "Margo Ledesma."

Her vocal caress swarmed through me. I understood her eloquent two-syllable, Spanish term of endearment. But it wasn't enough to stop me from hiding behind my pal's name when I shook her hand. "Cisco."

She cocked her head. "Your card says Leslie Soze."

"Nickname. My nickname."

As the cab turned onto the Great Highway, I cupped my mouth to muffle a snicker. She'd figured out before I did that I shielded my heart behind Cisco's name. It took even longer for me to realize she was too smart to sleep with me. But I fell in love with the perceptive psych major anyway.

Skirting the beach, I watched shards of moonlight dance upon waves toward the horizon. Salty air seeped in to replace the gritty odor of puddled asphalt. I anticipated Margo's signature scent—that of a breeze distilled by fresh rain.

Three

Dropped off in the gravel parking lot, I crunched my way into the lounge, clicking my Zippo. I hadn't phoned Margo about Pop until after his funeral and knew I'd hear about it. Craning my neck, I saw Margo perched upon a stool where the antique mahogany bar cornered left into the wall beside the jukebox. I slid my lighter into my pocket.

I wasn't much older than her, but in her sleeveless blouse and designer jeans, she looked like she never pushed past thirty. I didn't know if it was a function of my affection or if I was just an unrepentant dog, but the sight of her never ceased to spike my temp.

Weaving my way through the crowd, I watched her delicately sip her white wine. I never tired of her unpretentious grace. Fresh foam topped a frosty beer glass on the bar next to her. She'd kept faith with our custom of whoever got to our rendezvous first ordering for the other. I pointed when I pinched through. "That mine?"

She slid off her stool. "It is," she patted the seat next to her. "And this gives ya' a clear view of the exits. How'd I do?"

That Margo knew I felt better when the exits were in my line of sight not only didn't bother me, it settled me down, too. "Zippo's quiet," I said after an upside-down smile.

I leaned to hug her, and she threaded her arms around my neck. I buried my nose in her shoulder-length hair and drew in a fragrant breath.

"How's your mom and pop?" I said, sliding my arms from her narrow waist. We hiked up on our stools.

"Mom and Dad are still in Watsonville. Gettin' ready to retire."

"And your brother, Bobby? Married now to…Lydia, right? How are they doing?"

She squinted above a sly grin.

I knew that look. I laced my fingers around my beer, anticipating friendly fire.

"He's doing well. He finally went to the VA for treatment. Like you, he fought me about getting help. But ignoring his PTSD almost cost him Lydia. Love made him take his medicine. You should try it sometime."

"Love or medicine?"

"One will get you the other."

"Oh. You saying I got a chance with you if I get therapy?"

She snickered and then said, "I already love you. But from friendship's safe distance."

"Therapy then? Forget it, Margo. You talked me into it before, but I'm not going back to the VA to see another shrink…. no offense."

"That was six years ago when I was in the hospital. You couldn't turn me down," Margo honed in her glare. "But you didn't stick with it, Mr.—whaddaya call it? *Self-reliant*. And now this stunt of yours."

"Stunt?" I braced for her next shot.

"Hiding your father's loss until after his funeral. It not only tattles that you hide when you're wounded, but it upset me, too."

"You didn't say anything."

"You just lost him. I wasn't gonna be mad at you over the phone."

I jumped at a cheap deflection. "'Gonna?' When are you *going* to start talking like a PhD?" I'd kidded her about how she spoke, but she'd explained that when she came home from college, her blue-collar Irish mom and Mexican father were embarrassed that they couldn't understand what they called her *double-jointed lingo*. She'd decided she wouldn't *show off* unless she had to.

"Don't change the subject."

"You would've insisted on flying down if I told you before the funeral."

"Yeah. So?"

"You only met him a few times." I pictured Pop rising from his kitchen table to shake Margo's hand for the first time. "He couldn't get over your…what'd he call them—peepers." Pop's wry grin stretched across the scene in my head. "Yeah. He told me, *Don't let that one get away.*"

Margo gazed off into the distance. "My parents said the same thing about you after they found you asleep in my hospital room." She pivoted on her stool, her whole body faced me. "But I knew better. You still had too much of Bobby in you at that time. But that's history. I wouldn't have gone to say goodbye to your father. I would've been there to help you say goodbye."

"You make it unanimous."

"What?"

"DJ and Cisco said the same thing."

"Oh. An admission." Her lilt dropped into a digestive pause. "So, I'm not the only one you didn't tell."

Margo's slim finger traced the contours of her delicate chin. Then, some sadist punched up Neil Young on the jukebox. "*Old man look at my life, I'm a lot like you were,*" seeped through the chatter and clinking ice cubes.

I bowed my head. "I didn't want to bother you guys."

Margo caressed my forearm. "I can't imagine how hard it must be losing the parent who raised you."

I addressed my sweaty glass. "I'm fine. I'm getting over it."

She squeezed my arm, and I realized I'd cupped my other hand upon hers.

I looked up and watched her gaze rise from our hands to meet mine.

"*Mijo*, you just reached for my help."

I jerked my hand from hers, but Margo grabbed it back and laced her fingers through mine. She raised our woven fingers between us. "You need this." Her voice trailed like an invitation to follow.

Her warm touch softened the continued thumps of Neil's pensive lyrics. "Pop was dead by the time I got to him."

Her face pinched. "Is that guilt I hear?"

"I should've been there," I said as my eyes fogged over.

She squeezed our hands. "Do you feel your father blames you?"

I wiped the moisture from my eyes, but the guilt that bound me at the morgue ratcheted up. I exaggerated my scan of the bar and sucked in a breath. "Not here, Margo." I felt the gouge of Pop's chip on my shoulder and snapped, "Alright?"

She bit her bottom lip. "*Mijo*, the fact you opened up that much in this place says your grief is crying to be let out. Stuffing it only forces it to blindside you. Like those tears are now."

"I'm not about to dump my petty load on anybody."

Her worry lines fanned but vanished as quickly as they came. "There is nothing 'petty' about losing your father, and helping you through grief is what friends are for. I'm a psychologist and your friend, but if you won't talk to me, talk to Cisco and DJ. See another therapist."

She was right, but it was all I could do to take the simmer out of my voice. "You live up here. DJ lives all the way in Atlanta. Cisco is in New Mexico, busy with his new wife."

"You've no one to talk to in LA?"

"Nobody like you three. Those guys and me in Nam. You and me at UCLA."

Her voice dropped. "Cisco's walls are taller than I thought."

"Didn't I ask not to talk about it here?"

Margo pursed her lips. "It's nippy outside, but you're in a suit, and I've a down jacket. How about a walk on the beach?"

"And face your scalpel *mentis*?"

After a pinched smile, she said, "Come on, *mijo*. Think of it as a way of honoring your father."

She had me at that. I waved down the bartender and paid our tab. We left with me feeling like a kid braving for a polio shot.

As we strolled onto the moonlit sand, Margo laced her arm down mine and wove our fingers together. Our snuggled shoulders warmed against the ocean breeze.

"When you called, you mentioned that your father's funeral was quite an affair. Can you tell me about it?"

"Sure....I invited everyone else he knew, along with a couple of nieces, nephews, and his surviving cousins. Turned into a neighborhood reunion." Then I let slip, "Told my mom, too."

"Your mom?" Her shock spiked her voice and knocked us apart. But our hands held, and she quickly recovered a neutral tone. "I didn't know you had contact with her."

Mom showed up bleach blonde, wrapped in a fur coat, and sporting a new boyfriend. My pace slowed, and I stopped to face the surf. I let go of Margo's hand and stuffed my fists into my pockets. "I felt she should know."

She stepped in front of me and folded her arms against the cold. "All you've ever said was that you were a kid when she left."

"Yeah, Pop and I were pretty hard on her."

She tilted her head. "What made you say that?"

"Pregnant with me, she had to marry him. Don't think she knew how much he drank until they lived together."

Margo reached and coaxed my hands from my pockets, wove her fingers back through mine.

"By the time I started walking and talking, they were sleeping in separate rooms. I must've been in first or second grade when she began to disappear. When she'd come home, she'd chain smoke and pace like a caged lioness. I learned to keep my distance."

"I understand drinking pushing a woman away from her husband. But not from her—"

"I was daddy's boy. I'd chime in with bratty background vocals when he'd demand to know where she'd been."

"Still."

Still struck like a poke in the chest, but I realized that her challenge, like Pop's to my temper, wasn't meant to provoke a fight. Too late to knock that chip from my shoulder for Pop, I did for Margo. "One night, while she packed, Pop begged her not to leave us. I was only nine, but the bulk of her luggage told me she was going for good this time. When she stomped toward the door, Pop and I ran to block it. I glanced off the edge of her suitcase, ending up on my butt....Pop bent to scoop me up, and Mom bolted."

I untied a hand from hers and pinched the bridge of my nose to try and squeeze off that night's septic images. "I didn't see her again until I was a teenager. Can't blame her. We made her miserable."

Margo shifted her eyes back and forth as if seeing me for the first time. "No wonder you're still single. You're afraid the woman you love will abandon you. Like your mom." Her gaze drifted off then quickly returned. "I'd assumed that the war had made you skittish. Like my brother."

"Pop…Pop and I had her trapped." Why couldn't Margo see that?

"*Mijo*, you not only expect to be abandoned, you believe it's your fault."

Her words bore past Mom's scowl to churn up my ex's tears. I lost control of my tongue and mumbled, "Mom wasn't my only victim," then Linh Mai's stricken face sprang into view. Margo'd piqued my little girl's tomb. I gasped, dropped Margo's other hand, and grabbed my kinked belly.

"What socked you, *mijo*?"

I blinked away Mai's slain image and concentrated on my ex. "You made me think of Jessica, is all."

Margo stroked my shoulder. "See, you blame yourself for losing her, too. Isn't that why you're still single?"

Holding my stomach, I said, "All I know is nobody gets hurt if I keep to myself."

"You've never hurt me. Remember after my accident, you flew to San Francisco and slept in a chair in my hospital room? When I came to, there you were. My best medicine."

I squeezed my mouth. "The company was sending me to Frisco on a temp assignment. When I called to tell you, your mom answered your phone. Sobbing, she told me about your wreck."

"Oh, just a coincidence, huh?" Margo stepped so close her chin about scraped my chest as she raised her eyes to mine. "I know better. Your heart, not *coincidence,* plopped you in that chair. Now, the death of your father and your mom's appearance are breaking through your armor again. Shed it, and a friendship like ours could blossom into romance."

Whoa. I stumbled back as panic spiked my stomach. Had she dropped her guard? I couldn't resist if she did. But at the bar, she'd said she kept her distance. Still, I popped a warning, "*Saepe ignavavit fortem ex spe expectatio.*"

Margo cocked her fists onto her hips. "Now you've ducked behind your Latin BS."

"'BS?' I'll have you know that college students used to have to take Latin. It was presumed to sharpen the mind."

"That change of subject proves my point."

"I didn't change the subject. I said *Expectation based on hope has often disappointed the courageous.*"

Her eyes didn't leave my face. "I'm not talking about hope. I'm talking about opportunity."

Cornered, I droned, "Maybe I'm not ready to risk it." Then I stoked my voice. "By the way, my firm's moving to Frisco. Buying a high-rise on Market Street. We'll be neighbors."

Margo crossed her arms under her breasts. "You're just telling me now? That's some deflection."

I pressed to urge her to retreat. "Wanted to wait until it was a sure thing. I approved the numbers today. Our VP signed the escrow."

"Les, if you make me let you off the hook now, it doesn't mean I will once we're 'neighbors.'"

"Worth the break." I turned and stuck out my elbow. "Let's get out of the cold. And don't even think about billing me for tonight."

Margo threaded her arm through mine. "I owed ya'. You paid the tab."

Small talk settled my belly as we walked back toward the lounge.

"So, when do you think you'll move?"

"Targeting May first. We're buying the building where our NorCal office is located."

She gaped, but her lips quickly morphed into a grin. "April is next week. May will be here before you know it....You know, it's been years since you and Jessica broke up. Who you been sleepin' with?"

Was she fishing? I almost spurted,   *Jasmine*—but said, "Nobody." I couldn't tell her I paid for sex.

"No one?"

"Hey, at my age, sex isn't that important."

Margo halted but held my elbow. My momentum turned me into her glare. "Stop your nonsense."

"Okay, then who are you 'sleeping with?'"

"Uh-uh." She rocked her index finger in front of my face. "You know I'm not into sex for its own sake. This is not about me."

"Yeah…so I know some women who like to keep things simple."

"Sex without possibility."

"I suppose, but nobody gets hurt that way."

Resonating her voice in sync with her finger wag, she said, "How much longer do you think that heart of yours will let you get away with meaningless sex?"

"Hey, I'm off the hook, remember?"

"Only till ya' move here. Come on. I'll give ya' a ride to your hotel."

"A taxi is safer."

"*¡Ay tu!*" She swatted the air between us, adding, "Clinical cap off."

I slept little that night with my heart boomeranging between insisting Margo'd opened her door to romance and my brain asserting 'she's too smart for that.'

In the morning, I shared a taxi to SFO with the VP— listened to him bitch about the move. Then, I sat next to him on the plane, on purpose.

Four

Margo always insisted that I phone her after a visit to let her know I'd landed safely. But I'd waited too long. She called me after work the next day.

"*Mijo*, you make it home, okay?"

My heart fluttered to the sway of her voice, but fear of that flutter clipped my reply. "Yeah, yeah. Fine."

"Just checking—you sound tense."

"I'm fine, really. You caught me in the middle of a spreadsheet I brought home." I glanced at my blank CRT.

"Ya' work too hard. So, this is a good time to tell you that I have some surprises for ya' when you move here." Her voice pitched and rolled like a kiddie coaster.

Though titillated, I had to believe that whatever she meant was born of friendship. I coughed through the snag in my throat. "Like what?"

"Wouldn't be surprises if I told ya'. I've also been thinking that since San Francisco's rental market is so tight, if you can't find a place before the move, you can stay here till ya' do. You'd like my neighborhood, and you're gonna love the Bay Area."

Visions of my head upon a pillow next to hers burst about. I strained against those images. "Ah, thanks. I'll keep that in mind."

"Since we're gonna be neighbors, no more dead air. I expect to hear from ya', alright?"

I faked a chuckle, clinging to her term *neighbors,* not roommates. "I'll force myself."

"I'll pester ya' if you don't."

"I promise to keep you in the loop."

"Alright, *mijo.* Try not to work too hard. Remember, call me."

"Will do. And thanks." I hung up against an ache to tell her I'd stay with her. Turning on my computer, I mumbled, "She'd said neighbors, not lovers."

Hours of crunching numbers did distract me from my nagging heart and made me drowsy. Fading toward sleep, I shut down the PC. But in its dark screen glowered the charge that I'd be a fool to ignore a chance to marry Margo. I buried my face in my palms....It'd been her Platonic restraint that'd kept her safe from my hazardous heart.

I showered and then slouched into bed. Eventually, I stumbled into a welcomed sleep.

The faint wail of a little girl penetrated my slumber. I awoke in Vietnam, listening for the child's cry. But the snore of my Vietnamese counterpart stole my attention. I glared at his head, tilted back on a plump sandbag. It was the third time I'd caught the prick asleep on watch.

I hooked his nose with the flash suppressor of my M16 and lifted him. His eyes sprang open.

He scrambled up the bunker's wall until his head jammed the ceiling. I locked my gaze on his. Beads of sweat glistened upon his forehead.

An explosive flash slammed me to the floor amid shrapnel and splinters of jungle. Burnt powder fouled my lungs. Stunned and deafened, my body shook from the concussions that followed. Flat on my back, I gaped through the bunker's shredded roof at a lattice of sizzling red and green tracers. Scarlet flares floated above, signaling a perimeter breach.

Moisture mixed with the dirt on my face. Sweat? Blood? I couldn't tell. I didn't feel anything. I feared moving, scared I'd trigger pain paralyzed by shock. Afraid I'd shit in my pants.

Faint voices penetrated my ringing ears. Vietnamese. Ours or NVA? Were the voices getting closer, or was my hearing coming back? Again, a child's moan—*Linh Mai!*

I had to save Mai. Get to DJ's and Cisco's bunker. They'd cover me. I couldn't find my M16, but I patted my holstered .45. I lunged at my facedown comrade and shook him. "Come on. *Di di mao*, let's get the fu—" I felt something wet. Blood, goddammit—oh, man. Oh, man. Had I shot the sleepy fucker?

"You alright? Come on, man. Say something." He didn't move. I turned him over. Oh God, no. *Margo!* She's dead. Did I kill her? My bloody hand squished my mouth, and I spewed C-rat lima beans. Then, I heard Mai scream.

I wrenched the pistol from my holster and scurried like a roach through the ditch connecting our bunkers. Head first, I rammed into the boots of a dead GI. Crawling past, I came face to face—*Pop!* "God, no. Whaddaya doing here? Don't be dead, please don't be dead." I rocked him in my arms, my .45 flat against his back. "Wake up. Wake up. For God's sake, wake up."

A figure appeared at the edge of the trench and shouted in Vietnamese. I saw him snap an AK 47 to his shoulder through the smoky, moonlit haze. Whipping Pop's corpse between us, I aimed at my foe's heart. Our eyes met, and my trigger finger froze. My mother and I dropped our weapons and wept.

Jarred awake, my heart hammered my chest. Sitting straight up in bed, panting and soaked in puke, my head swam in the stench of bile and the lingering scent of spent ammo. I trembled in that position until the sunrise slit the blinds, and my body gave itself back to me.

I called in sick, unplugged my phone, and curled up on my bed.

By the time the darkness outside invaded my bedroom, I realized I hadn't eaten all day, and it didn't matter. I'd spent the day squirming in my sheets, untangling my dream.

Nam's nightmares always hemorrhaged Linh Mai but had never included my parents or Margo. But how Pop and Mom ended up in my dream made painful sense after Margo'd wielded her spade around my father's funeral. And Margo's death, maybe at my hands, added up to my fear that romance could kill our friendship. It hadn't taken Freud's wattage to figure that out.

I finally crawled out of bed and made it into the kitchen. After popping a couple of handfuls of dry cereal into my mouth, I went back to bed.

Five

I'd returned to work after my sick day, but haunted by my dream, only exhaustion bought me a few bumpy hours of sleep at night. Between losing myself in budgetary demands, I forced down a meal each day and neglected phoning Margo.

She eventually called and scolded me for not dialing her number. But I told her I'd been busy at work. Explained that our CEO insisted that our headquarters not only be moved but fully operational in Frisco on May 1st. That critical departments like mine were running overtime. I apologized for not calling but didn't tell her about my next trip to Frisco. Bleeding from my nightmare, I couldn't face her scalpel *mentis*.

I touched down at SFO with our transition team the following week. On our last day, two other bean counters and I took time to tour available real estate and apartments. I submitted several rental applications.

We stepped out of a Realtor's office clutching brochures, our blazers flapping in the breeze. We huddled on the busy sidewalk. Phil propped his hand upon his protruding belly and held up a property description. "These prices are extortionate."

Carlos crumpled his pamphlets into his inside pocket. "Quit crying. Your house is paid for. You'll sell it and make a mint."

"Yeah, but I'll never get near the house here for what I'll make off my old one."

"Neither will I, Phil, but we don't have a choice. We're too old to find new jobs."

Phil bobbed his head. "You know, Les here is lucky. He has no family to uproot and no house to sell. All he has to worry about is finding an apartment. Isn't that right?"

"I travel light," I said, though preoccupied with ditching them. During our tours, I'd quietly noted the location of a massage parlor. Its blinded windows and reinforced metal screen door suggested a sanctuary where I could escape my nightmare's ghosts.

Phil shot Carlos and me a conspiratorial grin. "You know what? How about we hit a North Beach strip club? Check out the naked ladies."

Carlos glanced at his watch. "It's not even dinner time."

"Ah, come on."

"Why not. Whaddaya say, Les?"

"No thanks. I'm going back to the hotel to review our numbers." Of course, I lied.

Phil elbowed Carlos in the ribs. "Let's go, Carlos. Les is either way too ambitious, or stripper bars are too tame for a wild and crazy bachelor, right, Les?"

"I've hit forty. My heart can't take it." I faked a guffaw.

Phil slapped the air. The three of us stood on the sidewalk, chuckling, eyeing the traffic for cabs.

"Here comes one." Carlos stepped off the curb and raised his hand.

I let them take the first taxi. Didn't want to arouse their suspicions since I was headed away from our hotel. I watched their cab cut a swath through the traffic.

I waved down another. Scooting onto the back seat, my dark slacks peeled up a strip of duct tape over a slit in the upholstery. Nice, I thought as I twisted to see the start of a gummy white scuff that must've striped my butt.

"Where to man?"

I glanced up from my contorted inspection but stuffed my aggravation. Instead, I hid my destination. "Garnet's Market over on Irving at—"

"That's on the other side of Golden Gate Park." The driver stretched his arm over his seat to face me. "There's a closer store."

The cabbie's shoulder-length black hair and goatee made me think I'd caught a failed rocker eking out a living in his shabby cab. "Ah, well, no. I'm meeting a friend there. Hey, where's the seat belt?"

"You're sitting on it."

"Here it is." I hiked my butt to grab the buckle. The cab hadn't moved.

"I gotta friend that works there. What's your buddy's name?"

I clicked my tongue. "Can we just go—does this buckle work?"

"Shove it in. It'll lock." He finally put the cab in gear and, defying angry honks, bullied his way between a pickup and a mommy van.

I jammed the buckle together. He swerved hard into a turn at the next intersection without a tap on the brakes. "Not very sociable, are ya'?"

"Nope." I braced to stay upright. My hands pressed into tape gum.

The taxi lunged from stop to stop, sped to the next, and then stumbled to a halt again. I could see him in the rearview mirror, sucking in his lips to keep from laughing as I rocked back and forth.

I glared at his reflection and noticed the large gap between his two front teeth. In silent retribution, I christened him Black Tooth.

After passing through Golden Gate Park, he sped to Irving and hung a right. "Almost there."

Parked in the market's lot, I paid the exact metered amount, including all my pennies. "Keep the change."

"Bet you squeak when you walk, too."

I got out, rubbing my tacky palms. Black Tooth chirped his tires to leave me gagging in a puff of smoked rubber.

Stewing against an urge to charge into the asylum across the street, I held at the Don't Walk light and pulled out my lighter. Click, click. As soon as the signal flashed green, I forced a stroll between the lines.

A locked, iron screen door blocked the storefront's alcove. I felt spotlighted by the transom's gleaming neon: *Lily's Spa*. Why couldn't the entrance be discreet? I pocketed my Zippo, rang the bell, and looked over my shoulders, afraid Margo might drive by. Not likely, but the risk bent my face toward the ground.

A horn blast spun my head around where my eyes collided with Black Tooth's. He pumped a thumbs-up as he crept by.

I fumed for what felt like an eternity before a harsh buzz announced the release of the screen's lock. As I slinked through, the front door drew open, revealing an Asian woman with high cheekbones, dimpled cheeks, and long, raven black hair. Her beauty snuffed Black Tooth's coarse image.

"Hello, you like massage?" stroked my eardrums with a suspected Vietnamese lilt.

"Yes, *cảm ơn*."

Her eyelashes fluttered. "You say tank you in Vietnamese. You speak my language?"

"No. Just remember some basics."

"Come." Her gaze didn't leave my face until I passed through the doorway, and she closed the door behind me. I guesstimated her age at just behind mine. Then I heard her chuckle and faced her grin.

"What you sit on?"

"Duct tape," I said as nonchalant as my clenched teeth allowed. "Any on my jacket?" I turned and craned over my shoulder toward my behind.

"No." She stepped in front of me, came close, and tilted her head. "You fight in my country?"

I balked at her intrusion, but a waft of her lavender scent subdued my alarm. "I made the trip."

"We take good care of you." Her eyes lingered before she turned and walked ahead of me toward a reception area.

I chalked up her gaze to curiosity. Following her, I enjoyed the subtle rock of her hips, which barely rippled her snug black cheongsam. Silky, floral highlights embroidered her dress. No other women were in sight.

A black couch, color television, and rosewood end table furnished the room. In one corner sat a Buddhist altar, backed by lacquer panels featuring a tranquil village scene. In front were offerings of tangerines, colorfully wrapped candies, and bundles of play money. Incense sticks glowed at Buddha's feet, their lazy smoke snaking toward the ceiling. Their sparkling fragrance tingled up my nose, replacing my hostess's titillating aroma.

Directed to a sign in sheet upon a wall-mounted shelf at the mouth of a hallway, I asked why I had to sign my name and if she'd check ID?

She sidled up to me and smiled. "Must have for business license, but I not 'check.' You like half-hour or hour massage?"

Uh-oh. She'd sought a commitment before introducing the talent. I always took an hour but only after choosing a woman that appealed to me. However, she'd certainly be my pick if available. "Are you my masseuse?"

"No, dear. I wish, but I manager and must meet customer. Do not worry, I have pretty girl for you."

Her tactful rejection tempered my disappointment, and I'd suspected, by her coy attire, that she was the madam. So, I believed her.

"Hour, please." I signed in as Cisco. She glanced at my name, told me how much, and I handed her cash.

"Come." This time, she strolled next to me down the hall. "Name, Kisko?" She stopped to open a door.

I followed her into a large, clean room with a Jacuzzi-jetted tub. "Not 'Kisko,' Cisco. The first *C* is like an *s*, and the second like a *k*."

"Nice to meet you, Cisco." She led me to a stack of folded towels on a chair at the foot of the linen-covered floor mattress. "For you bath." She picked out a hand towel for herself.

"What's your name?"

"Lily." She walked over and sat on the edge of the tub, where she started the bathwater. She waved me near to show me which button to push to kick on the water jets.

Aha, she must be the owner. But I doubted that Lily was her real name. Back in Saigon, the old sergeant who led me to my first brothel said, *Them girls ain't gonna give ya their real names. They need a shield to keep their whoring outta the rest of their lives. Same as us. So, don't give 'em yours.* That soiree was the first time I'd used my buddy Cisco's name. I didn't know then that I'd forge my crusty NCO's rule into a shield of my own.

I walked back to the mattress, where I started to undress, and heard Lily ask, "What you job, Cisco?"

"Accountant. CPA." Lily's back was to me, but as I draped my clothes over the chair, I couldn't keep my eyes from following the pinch of her waist into the contours of her supple hips.

"Where you go in my country?" Lily fluttered her fingers into the rising water.

"Mekong Delta." The ease of my candor surprised me.

Lily glanced over her shoulder to catch me naked. "Put towel on, bad boy." She quickly looked away.

"Sorry." I gulped, suddenly gripped by the possibility that the spa wasn't a front for sex. I grabbed a bath towel and wrapped it around my waist.

"Save for girl." She hadn't looked back.

With her deft reassurance that I'd get laid, she'd charmed me with her modest charade.

After a tentative glance over her shoulder, she held her gaze. "You been *Cần Thơ?*"

Her hometown? Why the peek behind her mask? Then, I felt a tug at Cisco's mask. That was it—wasn't it? This alluring madam had cast her hook. What better bait to reel in a repeat customer than to get personal. I should've been relieved by her bogus interest, but I couldn't deny a slight disappointment. "Never made it there."

"Cần Thơ, my home." She turned away and shut off the water. "Water ready. You like tea?"

"That would be great." Of course, she'd offer tea. I stretched a grin.

"I bring." She stood up and headed out the door, toweling her hands.

I strolled to the tub and lowered myself into the steamy bath. The temp, perfect. It tickled me that Lily'd said she'd bring the tea, not my masseuse. I humphed out loud—I should've been disappointed at the delay in getting laid.

After a tap on the door, Lily entered with the tea. Avoiding any intrusive gaze, she placed the foam cup within reach upon the flat edge of the tub. A Lipton label dangled over its lip.

"Thanks." I took a sip. The bitter taste betrayed no hint of sugar or honey. She'd brought no offense to my sanctuaries' customs.

She asked if I wanted anything else, adding, "Girl, come soon."

I shook my head and allowed my eyes to follow her until she dimmed the lights and closed the door behind her.

Upon completing my bath, I laid face down on the mattress. But images of how my high priestess of deliverance might appear kept bumping into the beauty and charm Lily'd packed into our brief encounter.

After a gentle knock, the door opened, followed by a mellifluous "Hello."

I lifted my head, stretching my eyelids to compensate for the stingy light. "Hi." Her silky hair ended at her waist. Her patent leather flats and black dress ended just above her knees, adding to her appeal. Despite the dull light, her honey-colored eyes glistened within their graceful contours.

"You come from work?"

"I'm visiting from Los Angeles."

She slipped out of her shoes and knelt beside me. "How you like massage?"

"Soft." I held my breath for her answer to my burns.

She introduced her fingers to my shoulders and detoured around my scars without a word. I surrendered to her touch. Like sparklers, her fingertips ignited my senses.

After kneading her way down to the soles of my feet, she permitted me to turn over. She smiled at a rigid Mr. Happy and asked what she could do for me. I humbly requested to enter from behind, anticipating the view.

"How much tip you give, honey?"

I didn't haggle and endured her departure to stash her cash by appreciating the genius of Lily collecting her licensed one-hour service fee up-front. What better way to insulate her from what goes on between the ladies and their customers? And it allows her masseuses to hide their exchange of money for sex behind benign tips.

When she returned, I sat cross-legged on the mattress opposite the pillow.

She stood before me and slid her dress's straps off her shoulders, allowing it to puddle at her feet. To my delight, no bra covered her perky breasts, nor did a V-string hide her shaven delta.

After unrolling a condom over Mr. Happy, she stepped in front of me, turned her back, and then drew her hands down her thighs before folding upon her knees to the mattress. She hugged the pillow and lifted her behind. I happily rose to my knees to greet her.

Caressing her waist down and across the spread of her hips, I drew my eyes down her valley, past orbital lips to those of her vertical smile.

She reached between her legs, and I beheld her grip on Mr. Happy as she ushered him through the glistening gates of her moist oasis.

Too eager at first, I drove Mr. Happy dangerously close to bursting his salvo. I caught my breath and slowed to a rhythm where my sighs merged with hers into a salacious duet.

Sweeping up into my heart's acceleration, my glide pitched into feverish strokes. Sweat seeped through my pores—a prelude to ecstasy's combustible end.

Passion crested, and I lunged out of control, greedily burying Mr. Happy. Euphoric spasms exploded from my body into hers.

Mr. Happy fell limp, contented.

My priestess collapsed on her stomach. I followed next to her and turned on my back. She graciously cuddled upon my chest.

After her brief snuggle, she excused herself to get up for a washcloth and went to the tub to soak it in hot water. She came back and gently cleaned Mr. Happy.

We dressed, and she took me by the hand to lead us toward Lily's reception area. Stopping at the sign-in shelf, she picked up a Lily's Spa business card and wrote her name. "You come back. Ask for Kim." She slid the card into my shirt pocket.

"I will." But I flashed on the night another masseuse's card fluttered to Jessica's feet. I'd bent down to untie my shoes. Jessica picked it up, and I'd watched the lines on her face twist from curiosity into confusion and then coil into accusation. Overcome with guilt, I'd confessed but told myself and tried to convince her that Mr. Happy had driven me to indulge cheap lust—that it hadn't meant a damn thing. Jessica's face had sagged under the weight of her tears as she pointed to the door and ordered me to *get out*.

Had my nightmare ruptured the seal on that fatal night? I dredged out Kim's card and shoved it into my pants pocket. Each time I'd reach for my keys, I'd touch and remember it. But Jessica hadn't appeared in my dream—Linh Mai cracked out of her tomb, accusing me of panicking after Jessica said I'd make a good father....I'd betrayed Jessica to escape seeing Mai's dying face in my own child's. I shuddered, dropping my gaze to the floor.

"You shake. You cold?"

I mustered a shallow breath. "Yeah, thanks."

Kim rubbed my arms, but desperate to staunch my bleed, I concentrated on Lily over Kim's shoulder. She sat on her couch, speaking Vietnamese to an Asian man who looked about my age. Lily looked up and addressed Kim in Vietnamese.

Kim glanced down the hall and then passed me a devilish grin. "Must go. Come back. See me." She sashayed down the hall.

"Feel better, dear?" Lily asked.

I cleared my throat. "Uh-huh."

The compact, muscular man on the couch scanned my face like I used to search tree lines in Vietnam. Stone-faced, he got up and strolled past me down the hall unaccompanied. I presumed he was Lily's bouncer. Former ARVN? Couldn't be NVA, right? Questioning his past helped silence my own.

Lily patted the cushion next to hers. "You have minute?"

"Sure," I said, though I'd nothing to be flattered about. Her invitation was aimed at my wallet. But better to nibble at her shallow hook than drown in my own depths. I walked over and settled into her lumpy couch.

"You live San Francisco?"

"Not yet." I'd decided that candor from my role in our charade was cost-neutral. "I'm here from LA looking for a place."

Lily slipped off her ballet slippers, brought her legs up, and folded her feet under her tantalizing derriere. She rested her arm atop the back cushion. "When you move here?"

Indulging her wile, I told her, "May."

"Soon." She reached over to pick a piece of lint off my coat. Her knee grazed my thigh. "What you remember in my country, Cisco?"

Her cozy touching and the tickle of hearing my bogus name tapped a longing I'd come here to evade. I reached for a memory suited to her game. "I and I."

Lily wrinkled her pleasant nose. "You mean R and R. When GI get leave."

"Hey, intercourse and intoxication, *I and I*, are all we cared about during 'R and R.' You know that."

She turned away, pulled the hem of her dress toward her ankles, and blandly said, "Maybe, but I not in same business in my country." She drew in a deep breath. The stretch of her upside-down smile couldn't erase Cupid's bow from her delightful lips. She bounced a playful slap off my arm. "Naughty boy. What else you remember?"

Her swat knocked free a dusty memory. "*Chôm chôm*. Used to snack on *chôm chôm* fruit in the boonies." I heard my words drift away. A diaphanous image of the lush Mekong Delta floated between us.

"Hmm, you learn my language. Eat my food."

Another vision formed with unexpected ease. "One time, we hacked into a clearing to find what I thought was a religious temple. Our Vietnamese scout explained it was a monument to literature. Even I couldn't miss the richness of a culture that built shrines to books."

Lily brought her hand back and stroked my shoulder. The pagoda vanished, leaving me staring at her long fingers.

"You see more than war in my country, Cisco. I bring something." Her *something* made me cock my ear. She hadn't missed the *h* to ting her *t* or pounded the *th* into a *d*. But she got up and scurried down the hall. I blew off her perfect pronunciation in favor of doting on whatever additional fluff she planned to tack onto retail sex.

Lily returned holding a dog-eared paperback. As she sat next to me, she smoothed her dress over her lap and laid the book there. With her hands bracketing the cover, she spoke as if introducing a sacred relic. "Here famous Vietnamese poem."

A burst of grisly images socked the wind out of me. I gasped, "Poem." I'd been ordered to rifle corpses for intel in Nam. All I found were family photos tucked between pages of loving verse.

Lily brought her hand to the back of my neck and pressed her soft fingers into my taut muscles. Her voice slowed. "You find poem on dead soldier. Happen a lot."

I shuddered in a broken breath. "It was a hideous way to discover your people's passion for poetry."

"Not you fault, Cisco." She kneaded the base of my skull. Her gentle touch began to tame my sputtering lungs.

"I'm okay….I'm fine." I forced my gaze to Lily's lap to read her book's title. *"The Tale of Kiều*, by New-yen Due."

"Not 'New-yen Due.' *Nguyễn Du*."

"'nWin You.'" Soothed by her touch, I focused on her book's black-and-white sketch of a waif playing a lute. "She looks sad."

"Because she in same business. But not always. Like me."

Her intimate disclosure should've made me bolt. But it sunk in that her book's title was in English. "You can read this?"

"Book in Vietnamese and English. It help me learn you language." Lily's fingers abandoned my neck to open her book, but she nuzzled her shoulder into mine. On the left page with numbered verses lay the original Vietnamese script. On the right, with corresponding numbers, were their English translations.

"See, you language and mine, next to each odder." Lily closed the book and squirmed slightly into her seat, nestling her thigh against mine. "You have Vietnamese girlfriend before?"

An impulse to run fell limp against the touch of her thigh. Left me struggling with how to say no to her question without dismissing Kim or other Vietnamese working girls who'd comforted me. I coughed into my fist. "Not really, but if the fire I felt with Kim is what it's—"

Lily's palm shot up between us. She covered her eyes with her other hand and bowed her head. "No, no. Between you and girl. I do not have to know."

Had she blushed? Impossible—she'd faked it. She couldn't acknowledge the fucking that went on here. She'd defended her deniability. Protected her business license.

Lily leveled an absorbing gaze to mine. "You married? Have girlfriend, Cisco?"

"Neither." Then I had to ask, "Are you married?"

"No longer." She averted her eyes.

Feeling her ache subverted my charge that she'd faked her blush. "What happened?"

"My husband like someone different." Lily stroked *The Tale of Kiều* with both hands, then picked it up and handed it to me. "Kiều in same business not because she want it. You take. Read. Maybe understand how I come here."

I couldn't refuse her book any more than I could now deny my attraction to her. I rested it upon my thigh.

Lily draped her arm over the back of the couch, leveled her gaze at me, and braced two fingers against her temple. "Cisco, when you come back, maybe tell me why you come here?"

An inner voice shouted, *My name is Les, not Cisco.* But luckily, before my tongue engaged, Lily stood up, smoothed the wrinkles from her dress, and said, "Kim give you number. Next time you come, call first."

My fear of infatuation popped out a deflection, "To make sure Kim is here?"

"'Make sure' I here." She shook her head and flashed me a crooked smile.

I glanced away but joined her standing. She slipped her arm through mine and walked me to the door.

Across the street at curbside, I gawked at her book. Puckering in a cool breath fanned the coals of my crush on the intriguing madam.

A taxi slipped past me. Shit, what if that had been Margo? I flapped my arms, and something flew out of her book. I chased it to the sidewalk and scooped up the photo. My gaze fell upon a young Lily standing alone in front of an all too familiar US Army hooch. Wondering if she'd left it there on purpose crowded out my paranoia at being spotted by Margo.

Lily couldn't have been more than a teenager. She wore sandals along with simple but elegant blue pants. Her white long-sleeve blouse, spotless. Her rich hair cascaded down her shoulders, ending slightly above her dainty breasts. Her left hand was raised above her eyes to block the sun, shading a meek grin that made her appear timid.

I gently wiped her photograph clean and waved down an approaching cab. Settled upon a soundly upholstered seat, I indulged Lily's innocent image.

The cab swerved around a double-parked van, and my thoughts tumbled back into Margo, chilling Lily's allure.

I'd ignored Margo's warning against hiding from Pop's death. She'd predicted my nightmare. It'd freed Mai to charge through Lily's doors. I had sacrificed Jessica to escape Mai. With heavy hands, I slid Lily's picture back into her book and then stared outside as we cruised through twilight-hued Golden Gate Park, the packed city's break from itself. I let my hobbled thoughts get lost in the park's lush greenery.

The day's jagged memories seized my thoughts again at my hotel room's desk. I shut my laptop and plowed my face through my palms. But Mai's painful image bled through.

I slapped my hands against the desk and pushed up. But I'd found no quarter at Lily's. I dropped back down with nowhere to run.

After forcing myself up, I flopped on the bed behind me. I grabbed the phone and ordered room service. Tried watching the news, but couldn't stomach the saber rattling against Panama. I switched to a less fatal sitcom only to be irritated by its laugh track. I punched off the TV.

After hardly touching the burger I'd ordered, I sat the plate on the nightstand next to Lily's book. Though I hadn't escaped my ghosts at her spa, Lily had resurrected kinder memories of Nam. I reached over and slid out her bashful image. I recognized that shyness—she'd blushed at my reflection on sex with Kim. It touched me that traces of her innocence had survived her trade.

I sat Lily's photo beside me and started reading what Du's narrative verse could tell me about her. Though intrigued by the epic poem, I soon dozed into a fitful sleep.

In the morning I called and changed my flight's seat assignment away from my colleagues. I couldn't be bothered explaining my reading selection.

Fasten seat belt sign on, seatback up, and I felt the clunk of landing gear locking down. The Boeing 737 bounced onto the tarmac and popped my nose out of Lily's book. I'd read that Kiều had been forced into prostitution by war and corruption. But that she'd held on to her decency despite her shame.

I let my head fall back against the seat. Why, of all the johns who passed through Lily's door, did she choose me to read Kiều's story?

"If you're stayin', let me out." Mr. Window Seat glared, hunched between me and the overhead.

"I'm going." I zippered into the aisle and snatched my carry-on from the bin above.

Steering out of long-term parking through the muddle of why Lily picked me, I supposed that she'd patted that cushion beside her out of curiosity over my Vietnamese *thank you* and that I'd humped the boonies near her hometown. Then I told her I'd snacked on *chôm chôm* and that a shrine to literature left an impression on me. That's when she'd said I'd seen beyond the war in her country. Had she thought I'd see beyond the madam in her?

Lily'd made it a point that she wasn't always in the sex trade....She'd lent me Kiều to tell me her survival had cost her her innocence.

That I'd confessed to rifling corpses seeped up as I slowed to a stop at a red light. But Lily's smooth fingers reached out of my memory and tingled up the back of my neck. She'd said it wasn't my fault....She'd seen that my survival had cost me my innocence, too. She recognized a kinship. I wanted to call her. Tell her I get it. That I see she's more than a madam.

I scanned the corners for a pay phone and dug my Zippo out of my pocket. Clenching it in my fist, I tapped my wrist atop the steering wheel.

A cacophony of horns yanked my attention to the green light. I punched the gas. Spotting a phone booth, I flicked on my turn signal. But its ticktock alerted me that it was Margo's talisman wrapped in my fist. That her death in my nightmare warned of our friendship's fate without its platonic restraint. I couldn't expose Lily's shattered innocence to a disastrous relationship with me. I canceled my blinker.

I silenced my lighter at my apartment and slid my key into the lock. After plopping my carry-on upon the coffee table, I sagged into my black leather sectional.

Taking a breath, I ousted Lily's business card from my pocket and pulled out my day planner to add her contact info. I scribbled her phone number under GYM and tore up her card. I'd call to let her know when I'd drop off Kiều. Then I'd disappear. And if Margo did relax her guard, I'd find the courage to tell her that being her best friend was too much to gamble on. That I'm not worth the risk....I heard her echo, *"Mijo, you not only expect to be abandoned, you believe it's your fault."*

Six

Our office manager buzzed me on a late Wednesday afternoon. "Les here."

"A Mr. Parsite on line one for you."

"Thanks." I'd been expecting his call. HR had told me Parsite called earlier to confirm employment.

"This is Les Soze."

"Mr. Soze, this is Archie Parsite. You recently gave me a rental application for one of my apartments in San Francisco."

"I remember."

"According to your app, you need it on the first of May. The problem is the current tenant won't be out by then. However, I have a flat in Noe Valley. It'll be vacant by then. Interested?"

"How's the neighborhood?"

"Desirable middle class. Pretty much anything you need is within walking distance. Lots of young families with kids and a fair share of mom-and-pop shops owned by aging hippies." Parsite chuckled and added, "It's not unusual to see signs in shop windows that say, *Closed to attend the Grateful Dead concert.*"

"What could be better," I said, though more a Santana fan. "How many bedrooms?"

"One."

"Okay. I'd like to see it. But I can't get there until Saturday. Is that a problem?"

After a brief silence, he said, "That'll be fine. Meet me at my office in the morning? Say, nine?"

"I can do that," I said, and he gave me his address. I'd fly up Friday night after work. Anticipation's spark at seeing Margo tempered against my vow to protect our friendship. I also felt the drag of returning Lily's book.

I opened my desk drawer. Next to my day planner sat *The Tale of Kiều.* Before calling my travel agent, I slid out Lily's irresistible photo. She'd be better off once I was gone. I tucked her image back between the pages and stroked Du's poem. My breath swooshed out through a rueful smile.

Cracking open my planner's calendar confronted me with seeing Margo while squeezing in meets with Parsite and Lily. Imagining myself facing Margo after handing Lily her book made me prop my elbows on my desk and brace my cheeks between my palms. My fingertips massaged my throbbing temples.

"Yo, Les." Carlos had stuck his head into my office.

My elbows splayed, dropping my chin dangerously close to my desk.

"Whoa. Didn't mean to startle you."

"No problem." I closed my planner. "What can I do for you?"

"Gotta question for ya' on the escrow's fund distribution."

As soon as he left, I tumbled back into the thicket of my scheduling dilemma. I pulled out my Zippo and took a stroll around my desk. Click, click.

Reception buzzed me. They were sending over the FedEx guy with a delivery. I was expecting another contract proposal, so I met him at my door and signed for the envelope. I started to toss it on my desk but stopped and stared at its glaring solution to the problem of Lily's book. It hadn't occurred to me to mail it. Shit, I wanted to see her again.

I flopped into my seat and put away my Zippo. I'd mail Kiều—but damn, I'd torn up Lily's business card. All I'd kept was her number. If I called for the address, she might recognize my voice. What would I say?...I tucked my tail between my legs and dialed directory assistance.

After noting Lily's address, my urgency to return Kiều faded. I could drop it in the mail anytime. I called my travel agent and booked a flight and hotel. The latter a place to come and go from to meet Parsite before seeing Margo.

Seven

At home, I plopped my briefcase on my desk and clomped into my galley kitchen, where I pulled a carton of milk from the frig. Startled out of a swig by my wall phone's ring, I grabbed the receiver, "Hello?"

"Sosayy, my man. Haven't heard from ya'. How ya' doin'?"

Shit. I hadn't spoken to DJ since after Pop's funeral. I'd told him I'd keep him in the loop about me and the move to Frisco.

"DJ, been meaning to call you." I slid the milk carton into the frig.

He chuckled. "Could die of old age waiting for your call. But..." his voice fell, "wanted to check on you. You moving on alright without your pop?"

"Doing okay." I'd no intention of laying out Pop's corpse from my nightmare. "Keeping busy with the company's move."

"When's that happening?"

"First of May."

"Next month."

"Yeah. Heading up there this weekend to check out an apartment."

"You must be as excited about moving near Margo as a kid at Disney's gates."

The glee in DJ's voice was nixed from mine by my decision to protect my friendship with Margo. "Yeah. I am." I dropped my arm and rubbed my thigh.

"Damn, that was underwhelming. Something happen between you two?"

"No, no. I am excited." My voice withered, "But…"

I heard DJ inhale and then exhale with a hiss. "Oh, man. Don't tell me Margo got married."

I gulped. "No, she didn't. But the last time we met in Frisco, she said things that made me think she might gamble our friendship on romance."

"'Gamble?' You've carried a torch for that girl since you met her. Not even your love for Jessica shrank Margo's real estate in that heart of yours. Why aren't you doing cartwheels?"

DJ saw through bullshit. In Nam, his conscience saved our souls as many times as Cisco's jungle literacy saved our asses. Though wary, I went on. "Part of it is, I can't figure her out."

"So, she didn't come right out and say you two should take that leap?"

"No. She didn't."

"What'd she say to bind you up?"

I sucked a breath through my teeth. "She thinks Pop's passing is a chance for, you know what shrinks say, healing."

"Yeah. But what'd she say about you two?"

I slipped my hand into my pocket for my Zippo. "On the one hand, she literally said she loved me from friendship's safe distance. Then, she turned around and said that Pop's death cracked my armor. That it's a chance for a friendship like ours to…to *blossom* into intimacy." Click, click.

"Hmm. I can see that leaving you up in the air. So, why didn't you ask her? She'd be straight with you."

"Ah." I tongued my cheeks. "The truth is if she is willing, she deserves better."

"What—what makes you so damned unfit?"

I felt the rustling of Mai's ghost. Margo'd want kids. "Maybe I'm not ready to settle down." I ached for DJ to leave it at that.

"I bought that shit back in your twenties when Jessica threw your whoring ass out. But you're not a kid anymore. You refuse Margo, she *will* find another man. And he'll pluck your friendship out of his marriage in a New York second. Then, I'll be stuck listening to you whine about it for the rest of your pitiful life. Something else has got you by the neck."

Images of my shuddering, brown-eyed orphan bled into my throat. I fell back against the kitchen counter.

"Les…Les, you there?"

Out of my mouth squirmed, "She'd want kids. It's not in me."

"What are you talking about? I saw how much you loved Linh Mai."

"Don't go there, DJ." My breath frayed.

"Oh man, you still blame yourself."

I pocketed my lighter and tried to pinch off agony's tears. "If I hadn't made us—"

"You 'made us' go to her orphanage because you cared about her. We'd come back from the boonies wore out, but you scooped up the toys you'd bought at the PX, browbeat donations out of the other grunts, and got the medics to drive us there."

I slid to the floor with my back against the kitchen counter. "There wouldn't've been a firefight if I hadn't made us go."

"It's not your fault. The nuns told us the VC left them alone. We didn't expect an ambush."

"I should've taken that bullet, not Mai." I hugged my knees to my chest and pressed my face into my hand. Rivulets sprang between my fingers.

"Les, not even the lord—" DJ's voice thickened before his words broke, but then coughed back coarse, "can control a stray round."

He'd watched Mai die in my arms. But he'd come home, married, and later had a daughter. I managed to stutter, "How... how do you look at Loretta with—without seeing Mai's face in hers?"

"Damn it, Les. I'm as haunted as you. But I bless Loretta for unlocking the love war denied us from giving Nam's kids. You got a choice. Keep your love buried with Mai, or let it loose on a new life."

I swallowed hard. "How'd you do it, DJ?"

"I let go of the guilt," he said slowly, but his words snapped back. "Pushed it back on the cruel motherfuckers who sent us there."

I pictured his jaw clenched, but what he said next rolled back gently. "Les, you have to do the same. Stop that guilt from robbing you of being your lucky child's daddy."

Could I let it go like DJ? I dared to close my eyes and envisioned a baby, Margo. She waddled toward my opened arms, her baby-fat arms swaying above her head for balance. Her warm embrace melting my guilty burrs.

I wiped at my tears before the glow of forgiveness. "Shedding my guilt won't betray Mai's memory?"

"That's what I'm saying. Hey man, why don't you come to Atlanta? See how easily Loretta lights up that heart yours."

Despite his tempting invitation, I couldn't go. "As much as I'd like to, I'm too caught up in the company's relocation."

"If that's an excuse to avoid me, you'll do it to Margo, too."

"It's no excuse," I sneered, but he knew me well. I calmed down. "I know, I know. I'm not above dodging either one of you."

"Margo know you're coming?"

I rose to my feet, turned and plucked a napkin from a stack on the counter, and dried my face. "Not yet."

"You gotta find out if she's willing to step up. And if she is, I don't want to hear that you turned your back on her."

I drew a long breath. "You're right, DJ. If she's willing, and I cowed, I'd never forgive myself."

"Call her right now. Ask what she meant."

"Give me a break. I will in person when I get there."

"Are you hearing your coward-assed self? Get her answer and call me back."

At least over the phone, she wouldn't see me shrivel if she denied dropping her guard. "Okay, okay. I'll call her as soon as we hang up."

"That's a promise, brother."

"I 'promise.'"

"Cool. You tell Margo your old partner DJ said Hello."

"I will," I said and hung up.

Intending to dial Margo's number, I lifted the receiver again. But my finger hovered in front of the square buttons. It took me a second to punch the digits.

"*Mijo*, I was about to call you."

My dread dipped below her bubbly greeting. "Ah, really?"

"Yep. Can't wait till you move here to ask."

I pictured her head rocking to her buoyant tone. Made me think of those surprises she'd mentioned before. "Ask me what?" I bellied up to the counter.

"Wontcha be up here by May first?"

"Uh-huh."

"Good. How'd ya' like to take me to San Francisco's Black and White Ball on the twelfth?"

My alarm garbled her bubbly tone. Was she asking as a friend or lover? Two years ago, she'd excitedly planned to attend with an MD she'd gotten serious about. Then, she'd called me the morning after. Choking back tears, she'd told me he canceled at the last minute, nobly citing a medical emergency. But her pals, a couple, ran into him at the ball. Her girlfriend had achingly described how the blonde upon his arm made it a point to introduce herself as his wife. That he'd sheepishly stood by as she proudly added that she'd *put her foot down and made him hand off a medical emergency to the on-call physician so they wouldn't miss the ball.* Margo'd sobbed as she realized that while she'd made love to him, he was merely fucking her.

"I'd like to," I said weakly and pounded my thigh.

"You'd 'like to?'"

"Yeah, really. I'm just confused. I mean, you were serious about that doc you'd planned to go with to the last one....So, ah, are you asking me as a pal, or—" I choked, coughed, and then hawked out— "did you lower your guard?"

"Look at you catchin' on," she said with a honeyed ripple.

"But at the Sunset Lounge, you said you kept at friendship's safe distance."

"That was before I'd seen opportunity shine through those chinks in your armor."

Margo's cadaverous face from my nightmare flickered back. "Yeah, well, without that 'armor,' I'm scared as hell I'll hurt you and lose you completely."

"Are you secretly married?" she quipped.

"Nooo," the stretch of my denial bent me at the waist.

"Then let go of thinking your love makes women miserable. And you know what? Lowering 'your guard' to admit your fears gives me more reason to lower mine."

I straightened up like an antenna struggling to pierce static. "How's that?"

"I'll be honest with you. After Dr. *Mentiroso's* lies, I found comfort in knowing that your affection is always true—despite my guard. So, when your grief broke through the wall around your heart, I saw our chance to defeat both our defenses."

My eager heart thumped. "Really?"

"*Mijo*, it took courage to expose your fears right now. Exactly what it takes to conquer your fear of intimacy."

I dangled my head. "I just spoke to DJ. Told him I couldn't tell if you'd lowered your guard or not. He insisted I call to find out. It was his cajoling, not my 'courage.'"

"DJ?" Then her voice patted softly. "That you talked to him about us is another example of opportunity's knock."

"It just came out."

"Like your grief did with me at the Sunset Lounge. *Mijo*, you're letting in the people who care about you."

But I'd tried to hide at Lily's Spa. "What if I panic and withdraw again?"

"Are you afraid if you do, I'll leave you like your mom?"

I palmed my forehead. "I dunno…maybe?"

"*Mijo*, isolating yourself is an old habit. I have mine, too. We'll both stumble along the way—step on each other's toes." She chuckled lightly. "How about we take baby steps until we gain our footing? We won't even say we're going steady."

Freed by her delicacy, my reckless heart spoke, "Think we'll be 'going steady' by the Black and White Ball?"

"I'm sure we'll be able to do more than that." In the wake of her suggestive tone, her voice swayed seductively. "After all, it'd be rude to betray the theme of this year's ball…*In the Mood.*"

Years of loving her sparkled throughout my chest. "Can't wait, Margo."

"There you go. Listen, we've lots to do. Gotta get you fitted into a tux and me into a gown. Things we'll do together. Baby steps."

Margo continued like a city booster. "We're gonna have a ball, pardon the pun. We not only get to dance to great entertainers in places like Davies Symphony Hall and the Opera House, but they put out gourmet snacks at the different venues that reflect the kinds of music we'll hear. On top of that, they put tents in the streets to accommodate even more culinary and musical delights."

I pictured myself cleaned up, arm and arm, with Margo in a sexy gown. "They close off Frisco's civic center except to foot traffic, right?"

"They do, and everybody wears tennies. It's a highfalutin block party. But now that you're gonna be a local. Don't call San Francisco, Frisco. It exposes you as a tourist.... Well, does your finger hurt?"

I shook my head. "From what?"

"Dialing my number."

I laughed. Told her my finger was just a little sore.

"By the way, you think you'll be staying with me until you find an apartment?"

My appointment to see Parsite's bit my gut. Made me want to admit that I'd been to San Francisco without seeing her. Explain that confusion and fear made me snub her. But what of my duck into Lily's? A jolt from Jessica's boot recalled that fatal confession.

Stroking my belly, I said, "Ah...that's why I called. Have a lead on a place. Flying up Friday night after work to see it Saturday. It's short notice, but are you going to be in town?"

Margo snickered. "Hold on, let me check my calendar.... You're in luck. My trip to Monaco was canceled. How'd you find it?"

"The company hired an agency." I grimaced at my lie.

"They tell you where?"

My belly knotted around her trusting tone, but Parsite had told me. "Noe Valley."

"Nice. The other side of town from my Cow Hollow condo, but the Mission District is next door. I run a Spanish-speaking group at the county clinic there on Monday nights. Wanna stay at my place? Then, Saturday we'll see the apartment together."

Parsite would leak we'd met. I'd have to keep him away from her. Straining the kinks out of my voice, I said, "No. No thanks. The company's paid for a hotel."

"Oops. My apologies. I've already outstretched a baby step. Stay at a hotel if that makes you comfortable. But my *platonic* offer stands if you change your mind."

"Thanks." But my warped relief that she'd shouldered the blame left me badgered by the trust it'd squandered.

"So, don't rent a car. I'll pick ya' up at the airport."

"Great," I said with forced enthusiasm and then gave her my flight details.

"By the way. Next time you talk to DJ, tell him I said Hello, and thank him for his 'cajoling.'"

"He'll like that. See you Friday."

"Meet ya' at the gate!"

I stared at the receiver after she'd hung up, frozen by my duplicity....I blinked at a muted ring, then jerked away at three harsh beeps followed by, "If you would like to make a call, please hang up, and try again. If you need help, hang up and then dial your operator." I slammed it into its cradle, but cramps doubled me up.

I hobbled into my living room to curl up on the chaise side of my sectional. The phone next to my couch blurted a ring. But I kept my hands pressed into my belly. Then my answering machine clicked on with DJ's press for an answer.

I couldn't call him back gasping against a spiking gut. I limped into the bathroom and flung open my medicine cabinet for antacids.

Back, curled up on my chaise, chomping chalky tablets, and keen for relief, I embraced Margo's deliverance from *going steady*. We'd no commitment to betray. Then it followed that her *baby steps* implied a grace period to bury the last ill-timed antics of a blundering bachelor.…My cramps began to fade. I'd reduced hiding Parsite and Lily from betrayals to remedial omissions.

Pardoning my secrets, I reached for the phone to keep my promise to DJ. While dialing, I boosted my enthusiasm by again picturing myself all dressed up, arm and arm with Margo. "Hello DJ."

"Margo, step up?"

"Hey, she's picking me up at the airport," I said in a withholding tease.

"You didn't answer my question."

I pumped pride into my glee. "She's making a *dream come true*."

"You free yourself to celebrate?" His tone matched mine. "Cartwheels?"

"Backflips." Told him I was taking her to San Francisco's Black and White Ball. An affair as elegant as we were serious about each other. I described the unique event.

"I'm going to need a picture of the princess and the penguin. So don't lose my address."

"You got it," I said and chuckled.

"And when you two tie the knot, forget Cisco, I'm your best man. He didn't make you call Margo." DJ's voice trailed in a chortling wake.

I stretched out after our call and kicked off my shoes. After sliding a tired throw pillow under my head, I closed my eyes to concentrate on an antiseptic scheme to keep Margo away from Parsite.

She didn't know Parsite's Saturday morning meeting time. I'd have her drop me at the hotel Friday night. Tell her to pick me up for an afternoon appointment on Saturday. That'd give me the morning to meet Parsite and get back before she arrived. When she picked me up, I'd tell her I'd already seen the place. Explain that the appointment had gotten moved back—early. That I didn't call to let her sleep in. My conscience pricked back. "How thoughtful," I murmured, recalling an old cowboy flick where the bandit used sagebrush to scatter his tracks. Effective, but the dust cloud soiled the crook.

I slid my fingers into my pocket for my lighter. Click, click.

Eight

As my flight leveled off toward San Francisco, I decided to toast the liberation of my love for Margo. With her meticulously cut chin bob, Megan, the flight attendant, took my order, "Tequila and tonic water, please."

She dipped her chin. "TNT coming up for the gentleman looking for a blast."

Chuckling, I sat back and closed my eyes, anticipating seeing Margo on the other side of friendship.

"Lower your tray table, please."

I unlatched it, and Megan handed me a plastic glass of ice, a can of tonic water, and a Cuervo miniature.

"Big thanks." I twisted open the bottle, emptied it over ice, and then splashed the tequila with tonic.

A fella a few rows ahead raised his hand and called out to her. Sipping my cocktail, I took in the incendiary swish of Megan's stride up the aisle until eclipsed by Lily's supple sway. I gulped my drink to drown Lily's intrusion.

On her way back, Megan couldn't miss me waving my empty mini. "I'd better order another."

She winked. "It pays to plan ahead."

Megan returned with a fresh glass of ice. After handing it to me, she reached into her apron pockets to bring out and wiggle a Cuervo mini from each hand. "Brought a couple. Pay me later. I won't charge you for the third if you don't use it."

"I'll need them both."

"A man who knows what he wants."

"That'll be the day." I took the minis and unscrewed one. Ignoring Megan's stride up the aisle, I hastily mixed my second TNT and belted it back. Ice cubes crashed into my teeth.

We began our descent about when I'd finished my fourth, or was it my fifth cocktail? Whatever the count, I gazed out the window. The sun had set, and city lights surrounded a moonlit pewter bay. My lofty hopes for Margo and me sparkled in sync with the glittering shoreline.

Jumbo tires screeched upon the tarmac in an otherwise smooth landing. And I was one of the first to reach the gate despite the effort it took to step straight against tequila's bend. I saw Margo threading through the crowd and shot up my hand in an excited wave.

Margo stepped through with open arms, wearing a cream-colored, deliciously tailored business suit. I sank my carry-on to the floor but noted Margo's jacket's mandarin collar. I flashed on Lily's cheongsam and winced.

"Something wrong?" Margo dropped her arms, looked down, and pulled on the hem of her jacket. Her purse's narrow strap fell from her shoulder, but a graceful swoop of her thumb returned it to her shoulder.

"No, no. Thought I saw something."

"What?" She kept checking herself.

I pointed at the ceiling. "Nothing. Must've been a shadow from the lighting."

Margo grinned and laced her arms around my neck. I wove my fingers together at the small of her back. But she leaned back, twitched her nose. "I smell tequila. How much?"

"Ah…lost count."

Margo folded her arms, and I released her. She stepped back. "That's not like you."

I toed the floor, glancing between her and my loafer. "I was celebrating seeing you under our new…paradigm? Guess I overdid it."

"'Paradigm?' That sounds like you. You sure it's not something else? I know you're worried about losing our friendship."

That worry had driven me to Lily's Spa. Of course, it'd wear her face. I met Margo's gaze. "I'll get over it."

"And I want to help you with that. But we should talk about it when you're sober. In the meantime, how about something to eat to shore up that shaky confidence of yours?"

"*Comida.* Good idea," I said, parrying toward tacos.

"You hinting at a taqueria?"

"*Si senorita. Vamoose.*"

Margo stammered between chuckles, "Gotta help ya' with your Spanish, too."

We headed toward the parking structure, and Margo asked, "How's LA these days?"

"Same-same. Except beaucoup congested."

She flashed a quizzical glance I couldn't explain but recovered. "Guess your move is keeping you busy."

"Oh yeah. You know. A CPA gets no quarter for pinching pennies."

More guffaws peppered our breezy banter all the way to her car. She opened her trunk, and I tossed in my carry-on.

We cruised out of SFO's spiral maze and dashed onto Highway 101. Margo's glance caught me taking in her sublime profile.

"Whaddaya staring at, *mijo?*"

"'At' how lucky I am."

"Aren't we both." After an encouraging smile, she went on, "I know a taqueria in the Mission District. It's near the county clinic where I do group. I'll point it out to you."

Minutes away from her clinic, we strolled into the taqueria. Against tequila's fading buzz, I took control of my thoughts and yukked it up with Margo over tacos. Not even our shaky table's stiff plastic chairs distracted me from Margo's lithe manner. I found her sexy without a touch of vulgarity. By the time we meandered to her car, I'd was kicking myself for not staying at her place.

It wasn't until we turned toward my Union Square hotel that she mentioned me opting for it instead of her condo.

"Hope you're comfortable there, *mijo.*"

"You know me, didn't want to put the boogaloo on ya'."

Margo shook her head. "'Boogaloo?'"

"Yeah, hassle you. In Nam, we called it the boogaloo."

She puckered her lips. "Earlier, you used *same-same* and *beaucoup* when I asked about LA. I haven't heard you talk like a…what'd they call you and my brother in the Army—*grunts!* That's it. I haven't heard you talk like a grunt since UCLA."

I and I—R and R lit my skull like Lily's neon. Meeting her must've dredged up my GI jargon. My cheeks flushed prickly as I watched Margo steer through the clogged traffic. Would she spot my guilty burn?

She double-parked in front of the hotel and turned to me with a knitted brow. "I get the hotel. Gives you a safe distance for us to start from. Your drinking, too. Neither are rare responses to anxiety. But your lapse into Army slang. That's a surprise."

She'd caught Lily's scent, but a knock at my window startled me. I turned to face the hotel doorman.

"Sir, sir. Are you checking in?"

"Saved by the guy in the funny hat," I said to Margo as I rolled down the window before answering him. "Yes. Yes, I am."

"May I help you with your luggage?"

I grabbed the door handle. "No thanks." I turned back to Margo. "Time for a nightcap?"

She jutted her chin toward my grip on the door. "You sure you want me to come in?"

I glanced at my grip and let go.

Before I could speak, Margo dropped her gaze. "I have to own my own ambivalence, too." Then she quickly lifted her eyes to mine. "Not about us, but toward exploring what brought up your GI slang."

I watched her chest swell with a laden breath as my lungs froze for what might come next.

"When Bobby came home, he drank a lot. He broke down once and described some of the gruesome things he—" Margo cleared her throat. "I can deal with your fears about risking our friendship, but your Army slang tells me to prepare for war's grisly details."

She pressed her lips together, and I watched her strain pull at the corners of her mouth. "Maybe tonight we should take a rest. I'd like us both to be ready to talk. You know, when I'm prepared, and you're sober and willing."

"Tha—thanks, Margo," I said, but recalled Lily hadn't flinched talking about the war.

"So, that brings us to tomorrow. When's your appointment?"

Her voice's innocent flutter stirred my guilt over my scheme to keep her away from Parsite.

"One."

Margo patted my knee. How about I pick you up at noon? That'll give us time to find parking and make your appointment. Afterward, maybe we can talk about what 'the guy in the funny hat' saved you from?"

"Can't we forget him?" I fumbled my words like a kid dreading being found out.

"Don't worry. I'll only put on my clinical cap if you let me."

"I have a choice?"

"Yes, you do."

"I'm still intimidated." I hadn't lied about that.

Margo grinned and offered her cheek for my goodnight kiss.

I pecked her cheek, hit the curb, and snatched my bag from her trunk. Waving as I watched her inch her way down the street, my other hand grabbed my lighter.

Nine

I taxied through Saturday morning's thin traffic for my nine o'clock appointment with Parsite. While I took in his Embarcadero office's impressive bay view, he slipped a blank lease into his briefcase.

Cruising in his two-seater Benz, he drove us past a row of San Francisco's Painted Ladies. Their ornate Victorian and Edwardian architecture popped with their multicolored highlights. In Noe Valley, it tickled him to point out the small shops he'd seen "Closed to attend the Grateful Dead concert."

He also taught that city housing didn't guarantee a garage. An offense to a native Angeleno raised in LA's car culture. A wound salted by stingy street parking that put us blocks away from his vacant flat. I might've caved to his offer to rent a garage if I was still a kid driving my *cherry* fifty-six Chevy. But I'd let my bland import defiantly tough it out.

His one bedroom's cheerfully painted Victorian was a little too flashy for me, but I liked its compact neighborhood. Though smaller than my LA apartment, I wrote him a check to seal my May first move-in date.

Though getting late, I thought I had time to beat Margo to the hotel and accepted Parsite's offer to drop me off.

Snailing through the thickened traffic, I'd been fooled by the morning's quiet streets. Apparently, drivers didn't sleep in that late on Saturdays. I jumped out of the Benz just before noon and tromped into the hotel lobby to the clicks of my Zippo. Relieved I didn't see Margo, I sank into a leather club chair.

Margo strolled in moments later, wearing enticingly fitted jeans and a floral silk blouse with only its top button unfastened in tasteful restraint. I put away my lighter and walked over to greet her while silently rehearsing my best *Aw-heck* act that I'd already seen the apartment.

We hugged and kissed each other's cheeks before she raised her watch for a glance. "Ready to go?"

"Um…I've already rented the place."

"What?" Her wrist dropped.

"Yeah, the landlord called and moved our appointment back. I didn't want to bother you so early, so I went by myself."

Margo looked around as if checking for eavesdroppers and poked her chin toward where I'd been sitting. "Come on. We need to talk."

"You said I had a choice."

Her face pinched. "This is about why you went without me. Not your lapse into Army slang."

That I'd wounded her raked up her limp body in my nightmare. I plodded behind her but helped her scoot together two club chairs.

As we sat, she pointed to mine and said, "It's not Freud's couch, but it'll have to do."

Margo planted her elbow upon the arm of her chair and braced two fingers against her temple, just like Lily. I cringed.

"You flinched." She leaned forward, braced by her forearms upon her thighs. "You want to tell me the real reason you went without me today?"

She deserved to know that I'd snuck into town behind her back. I squirmed in my seat, anticipating the damage from explaining that I'd hid to escape fears struck by a nightmare. I heaved a sigh…."Margo, after the last time I saw you, I had a nightmare about Nam." My muscles gave to sink me further into my seat. "You, you were in it."

Margo sat back and laced her fingers tightly together upon her lap. She swept her gaze about the lobby only to have it fall. "Maybe we should wait for a private place to talk. Baby steps, right?"

I imagined she'd strained her retreat from *war's grisly details.* "'Right,'" I said, forsaking my confession that I feared I'd killed her in my dream. I forced an indulgent smile against a nagging disappointment in her retreat. "How about I show you my new place? Then lunch is on me."

"You got the keys?"

I injected her ready relief into my voice. "Yes, ma'am."

"Okeydoke, let's check out your new *casa*."

I led Margo on Parsite's route through Noe Valley. We both chuckled at the neighborhood shops I'd been told locked up to attend *Dead* concerts. Margo cheerfully added that despite San Francisco's perch at the tip of a narrow peninsula, Noe Valley was but one of "A menagerie of unique neighborhoods that we'll never tire of exploring."

After searching in ever-expanding circles, she found a tight place to park blocks away. "At the risk of stating the obvious, parking is always a hassle in this town," she said as we began our hike.

"Ran into that this morning." Though we kept our chatter light, I did dread she'd rap on my nightmare's door in the privacy of my new place. I reached for my lighter. Click, click.

Margo slowed and gently pressed her hand upon my wrist. "I wondered if I'd hear that." She faced me, stopping us on the sidewalk. "*Mijo*, remember I said we'd step on each other's toes?"

I squeezed my Zippo. "Yeah."

"I broke my promise to let you choose to talk or not this morning because I felt rejected."

"I'd hurt you."

"We both stumbled," she drew back with a confident grin. "No more than clumsy baby steps. I'll forgive you if you forgive me."

"Of course," I said, adding, "So it's up to me to tell you about my nightmare?"

"How about I help you decide when you're ready to try." She reached for my hand.

I almost countered with, *How about when you're ready?* But didn't as I slipped my lighter into my pocket and took her hand. We resumed our stroll to my empty apartment.

Margo stopped to admire my building's lively colors. "These dolled-up Vics are somethin', aren't they?" Then she pranced up the steep steps.

"Nothing like them in LA." I followed and unlocked the door.

Inside, she pointed out the apartment's crown molding and polished hardwood floors. She even liked the kitchen's ancient but pristine Formica countertops. "Good as new." She clicked her nails across their faux-marble finish.

I traipsed behind her, lifted by her breezy commentary. At the end of our tiny tour, we sat on the bay window seat across from the fireplace. Margo pressed her hands down next to her hips and wiggled her delightful butt. "You're gonna need cushions. Let me help ya' pick 'em and fix up the place."

"Deal."

"All your old furniture gonna fit?"

"Not likely." I knew what was coming.

"You going part with your bleak, black sectional?"

She never liked the color, but I sank into the thing. "Have to see if it fits first." Lily's lumpy couch popped out of my memory. I spun off into how to wrestle my monstrosity into its new compact living room.

Margo clicked her tongue and bumped her shoulder into mine. "You hungry yet?"

"I am. Remember, my treat."

"In that case, there's a great crab house over in the Sunset District. Whaddaya say?"

Shit. Lily's Spa sat in the Sunset. I bet Lily liked crab. What if we ran into her? "Isn't that across town?"

Margo bobbed her head. "You've been studying maps. It's a ways."

I cleared my throat. "I'm starving. How about someplace closer?"

"Okeydoke," she puckered her lips…."I know. John's Grill. Home of the Maltese Falcon."

"Dashiell ever eat there?"

"He did."

"Seriously?"

"Yep. It's been around since 1908."

"Sounds cool. Where?"

"Near your hotel."

"The company's new building isn't that far from there. I'll show it to you after lunch."

Inside the grill's wood-paneled walls, busy with framed VIP customers' photos, and far from Lily's, my appetite showed up. I ordered lamb chops in deference to Sam Spade, and Margo opted for their filet of sole. And what better potion to numb my conscience than a bottle of fine Napa wine?

Between bites, Margo challenged me to a game of identifying celebrity pics. She caught the likes of Lauren Bacall and Sophia Loren. I managed to spot Willie McCovey.

While we shared a slice of New York cheesecake, Margo said, "*Mijo*, May is coming up fast. I've got my eye on a couple of gowns for the Black and White Ball." She slipped her dessert fork next to the plate, lit those emerald eyes upon me, and dipped her head. "You wanna help me pick one after we see your new headquarters? We'll find ya' a tux, too."

My impatience with shopping melted in her glow, and I gladly agreed when she said we'd shop in nearby Union Square—far from Lily's. But I couldn't help peppering my glee with playful sarcasm: "Oh boy, shopping."

She folded her arms across her chest and glared. "I know 'shopping' annoys you. But it can be fun."

"For you," I muttered.

She slapped my knuckles, then said, "Come on, show me that new building of yours."

Margo pointed out the Bay Bridge and Treasure Island through the top floor's wall of windows. Then she turned to me. "Your office gonna be here?"

"Are you kidding? CEO gets this view. I'll be on the floor below next to the CFO's office."

"'Kidding?' We do have to boost your confidence."

"I know what will. Watching you slink in and out of sexy gowns."

"*Ay perro*, don't be be such a dog." She grabbed my hand. Let's go see your new office."

Margo looked out my office's meager window. "This is cozy, and you have a partial water view."

"You're being generous. It's so cramped that after I squeeze in a desk, I'll have to step outside just to change my mind." I reached for the door. "Let's go see the rest of the place."

Margo slid her hip between her thumb and long fingers. "Now that I know where to find you, I've seen enough. Come on, Fido, and I'll let you watch me slip into something sexy."

"Ruff, Ruff." I swung open the door.

Holding hands we strolled toward Macy's and stopped at a flashing Don't Walk signal. At a lull in the traffic against the light, Margo pulled me off the curb to cross the street. We weren't alone. "What the—"

Looking over her shoulder as she tugged me along within a swarm of other defiant pedestrians, she grinned. "Get used to it. This is how locals deal."

I looked back at the law-abiding, still at the curb. "Tourists?"

"You catch on quick."

Safely on the opposite corner, I said, "So, locals defy traffic lights when the odds seem in their favor."

Margo grinned. "I should warn you about driving, too. Unless there's a car in the way, don't make a complete stop at a stop sign. Your back bumper is liable to get tapped by a local. Everybody just slows to a crawl without stopping and then shoots across."

At the next intersection, everybody held at the curb as a taxi barreled through. I caught the menace's profile—Black Tooth. I watched him fail to bully into the next lane. He slammed on his brakes behind a double-parked van.

"Time to go." Margo pulled me off the curb, interrupting my disappointment at the grip of Black Tooth's brakes.

In Macy's women's department, I saw that Margo'd had her eye on more than *a couple of gowns*. I threw up my arms at her third, floor-length selection. "Whatever happened to miniskirts?"

"*Cochino.*" She stomped off the pedestal, pushed aside my raised hands, and then swung down to pinch my ribs. "Don't be nasty."

Both chuckling, she marched off for yet another selection. But I could've watched her step on and off that pedestal all day before Macy's tall mirrors. I enjoyed her graceful turns to me, for my opinion, as she smoothed the rich fabric over her flat tummy.

Without buying a thing, she dragged me off to traipse from one grand department store into the next specialty shop. I delighted in her attention in an exclusive men's shop as I tried on tuxes. But when I rejected a pink cummerbund, she wagged her finger. "Now you're being macho."

When I whipped out my credit card for an outfit I liked, she nixed it. Not because she didn't like it, but because "There's more to see. We'll circle back if we don't find a better one."

We did end up circling back for that suit and to Macy's for one of the first gowns she'd slipped into. And I'd learned that to *shop till you drop* was no empty cliche. By dinner time, my tired feet clomped the couple blocks to Margo's favorite Japanese restaurant.

Inside the subterranean sushi bar, Margo recognized my puzzled look at arrays of raw fish floating by on small boats within a circulating canal. "Take what you want. Each bite is served upon its unique pallet. They charge by that plate."

"Uh-uh. Not without seeing a price tag."

Margo put her fists on her hips. "I'll buy, Mr. CPA. Sit and enjoy."

I passed on dessert behind my stack of porcelain pallets. But when Margo slowly slipped her spoon from between her lips, leaving a smooth mound of green tea ice cream upon its tip, she pointed the shiny dollop toward my mouth. "Have some?"

I devoured her sexy invitation. "So, baby steps mean baby fed, too?"

Margo giggled. "Look, if I'm not keeping you from one of your *chicas* who *keep things simple*, there's a combo playing in Berkeley I'd like to hear. Wanna go?"

"Whoa, where'd that come from?" I blurted though Kim's face glowered out of my conscience.

Margo raised and twirled her dessert spoon. "Just a nudge in case you haven't gotten around to cutting them loose."

I took an advance from my postal plan to snip Lily's tether. "There are no other '*chicas*,' Margo."

"Music then." She started digging through her purse.

I pulled out my wallet. "No. Take my—" but Margo pushed my hand away before I spouted *dust!* Slang for money in Vietnam. I imagined swiping my brow.

"My treat, Remember?" Margo handed the waitress her a credit card.

On our way to Berkeley, I envied Margo's uninhibited description of her band's fusion of Mexican music with rock and roll. Made me look forward to putting Lily behind me. Toward yakking without having to redact bachelorhood's dicey debris.

Inside La Peña Cultural Center, the performance didn't disappoint. And it didn't take but a couple of songs and my appetite for more of Margo's rhythmic sway to let her pull me onto the dance floor. Her signature samba dazzled before the spectacle of my stilted steps. But when the band slowed into a doo-wop classic, our embrace dancing to "Silhouettes" lit up my night.

Rapt in affection for Margo, I danced with her through the end of the combo's last encore. Hardly felt the nighttime chill on our stroll to her car.

As we curved onto the Bay Bridge toward San Francisco, Margo waved her hand next to her cheek. "Whew. Can't remember the last time I danced that much."

"I never have. If you call my bouncing around dancing."

"Oh, stop. I can't wait to dance with you at the Black and White."

I imagined us snuggled into a slow tune at the ball. To a song we'd make our own.

When we arrived at the hotel, she turned to me. "Too bad you have to leave tomorrow night."

I would've liked to have agreed, but a paranoia over bumping into Lily pricked back. "I'll be back soon, for good." I'd sever Lily's tie by then and never again have to mislead Margo.

Our lips met over her console in a sweet but fleeting kiss goodnight.

"How about breakfast in the morning?"

"Great," I said against my dread of running into Lily.

"Pick ya' up at nine?"

"Perfect." I wished I'd booked a morning flight.

I dragged myself out of bed in the morning and into the shower. Leaning my face into the steamy spray, I imagined last night's cuddle-and-sway with Margo. I looked forward to seeing her. It occurred to me that Lily's professional obligation to honor anonymity would prevent her from acknowledging me in the unlikely event we ran into her. I shouldn't be worried about anything but the slip of my own Freudian tongue.

Dressed and packed, I focused on tasting Margo's lips again. I strolled into the lobby just before nine. Stepping up to check out, I met the hotel receptionist's mandatory smile with my sincere, sunny grin.

Margo soon arrived and drove us to a hip Haight-Ashbury eatery. After breakfast, she saddled us onto a carousel ride in Golden Gate Park, tapping us into a gaggle of giggling youngsters. I couldn't help but feel the kids' infectious abandon.

Arm in arm away from the merry-go-round, she surprised me with a visit to the Academy of Sciences' *Far Side* exhibit. San

Francisco's whimsical sense of humor extended to an entire display of Gary Larson's work. I chuckled over the room's centerpiece, a giant microscope.

The afternoon slipped away in the park's rich array of galleries and gardens. By the time our empty stomachs demanded attention, we had to wolf down our bulging deli sandwiches as Margo sped toward the airport. Despite the time crunch, I felt we both floated into SFO on high spirits. But without enough time to walk me to the gate, Margo nudged her way to the departure curb to drop me off. Neither one of us had brought up my nightmare or my GI jargon.

"Next time, I'll be leaving home from here."

"You're not gonna want to leave." Her eyes glistened as she gave me a smack on the lips.

"Hard to go now." Still focused on her lingering smile, I forced myself to grab my bag from the back seat and sprinted to the gate.

Closing my eyes in my assigned seat, I packed my head with images of Margo slipping in and out of her sexy gowns and then me devouring her dollop of ice cream. In the inertial press of our ascent, I relived Margo's snuggle against my chest during our slow dance's heated embrace. A grin melted into my face.

Unpacking at home, I commended myself for surviving my first clumsy steps toward romance. I opened my desk drawer to shove in my planner only to confront *The Tale of Kiều.*
I sat and cracked it open to Lily's picture, ready to scold her for interrupting my time with Margo. But I stalled in her innocent stare, reminded that she'd revived kinder memories of Nam. "Along with my GI jargon," I snorted and shook my head.

Focusing back on her shy photo, I felt her gentle touch ease my conscience for violating corpses. Heard her forgiving voice say that it wasn't my fault—she hadn't faltered at my confession like

Margo did at my nightmare. Intent to stop Lily's intrusions, I closed the book upon her photo, exiled Kiều to my file cabinet, and locked it.

Lumbering into my living room, I traded my cabinet key for my Zippo. The smooth edges of Margo's talisman, a reminder of our years of friendship. I settled into my sectional and visualized our time to come as a couple.

Ten

The movers, Chuy and Floyd, had loaded my things in LA. Their overalls' name patches reminded me of Pop's embroidered over his heart. I kept rubbing away insistent tears.

In Noe Valley, against their protests, I helped them haul in boxes. Then, I watched them squat down to grip the ends of my couch and lift the monster off their truck.

I sank back into my living room doorway as rotund Chuy, craning his neck to look back over his shoulders, tentatively shuffled backward through the front door into the hallway.
"Hall's too narrow," Chuy huffed. "Can't turn into the front room."

"Go straight back till I'm in there," panted Floyd, climbing the steep stairs outside. Lanky Floyd struggled to raise his end level.

Wafts of BO fouled my nose as Floyd made it in and trudged by me. "Set it down. Take a break," I said.

"We're fine," gasped Floyd. They gauged the sofa's length against the tight angle into the living room.

"You going to be able to make that turn?"

Chuy cocked his head at me to make way. "Step aside. Watch us work our magic."

I flashed on Pop, leaning back from under the hood after fixing my stalled Chevy. *It'll start now,* he'd said. It fired right up. I pinched back tears while hugging the hallway past Chuy.

The pair wrestled with that damned couch. Through a series of fits and starts, peppered with Spanish and English curses, they angled, tilted, and squeezed it through. I followed and kept quiet about the paint chips littering the doorway floor.

"Where you want it?" Chuy panted. They held it with its back to the bay window.

I preferred to face the window but couldn't risk any more damage to my security deposit. "Perfect right there." Besides, my bookshelves would fit better across from it on either side of the fireplace.

They had an easier time lugging in the chaise section and reattached it to the beast. The bookshelves came easily.

Floyd slipped off his Dodger cap and dragged his forearm across his glistening brow. "Pardon me for saying so, but for a guy with not much to move, that's one helluva sectional." He looked around the now-crammed living room. "Takes up the whole place."

I shrugged. "My old place was bigger."

"Guess I shouldn't complain. At least you got one fat piece. We get paid by the pound, ya' know."

Without meaning to, he'd noted how cheap my move had been for the company. I'd culled my furnishings in LA, including all my office furniture. I probably should've sacrificed the couch, too. Margo would've liked that.

After the sweaty pair tromped back to their rig for the last time, Pop's achingly sweet memories continued to float upon my appreciation for their pride in their work. I wiped my eyes and opened all the windows to a nippy breeze to air out the place. Surrounded by needy boxes, I sank into my sofa and decided to open the box next to me.

Staring back from the opened flaps, three slacking teenagers in jungle fatigues leaned against an APC. Cisco, DJ, and me carelessly held our M16s. I snickered at our defiant smirks — all we had against our flimsy futures.

Finding where our pewter-framed photo belonged on the fireplace mantel took me a minute. I properly adjusted its angle.

Stepping back for a final inspection, Lily's teenage image burst to mind. My cheeks puffed like a blowfish, only to deflate with a hiss. I'd ignored her in favor of the move. Time to tie up bachelorhood's loose end.

"Okay, okay. Where'd I pack her book?" I glanced at my watch. After six. Margo said she'd be here to help unpack between six and six-thirty. What if she found *The Tale of Kiều*—Lily's photo? My thoughts shot from one dead end to another. So I had a book? An old pic. So what! So what? She'd connect them to my GI jargon.

Combing my fingers through my hair, I remembered stashing *The Tale of Kiều* between sweaters. But I'd labeled my boxes by room, not contents. Sweaters were labeled *bedroom*. Throwing up my hands, I lurched through a maze of boxes and stumbled into the bedroom. Drawing the blade of my Swiss Army knife, I sliced through a taped seam of the nearest box, but the doorbell's ding-dong shuddered my lungs—Margo?

I caught my breath before reaching the door, but grasped at excuses to keep her out of my bedroom boxes if it was her. I gulped, opened the door to Margo, and swooped my hand toward the hallway. "Come on in."

Despite her fashionably bulky sweater, the contours of her waist filled the mouth of her snug jeans beckoning my eyes to follow as she passed. A welcomed distraction from my clash with Kiều.

She held out a gold, organza gift bag. "Welcome to San Francisco."

"What's this?"

"A housewarming present."

"First, *dame un beso*." I spread my arms.

Margo laced her arms around my neck as mine threaded her waist. Our lips met and opened to our first long, tongue-bathed kiss. But when our bodies stole together and lit against restraint,

Margo slid her hands down my arms, leaned back and fanned her cheek. "*Ay, qué rico, pero*—baby steps. Remember?"

I reluctantly relaxed my arms, and Margo stepped back. She raised her present between us. "Hope you like it."

I took her gift, started digging through scarlet tissue paper, and surrendered my simmer to a fancifully carved, flaming orange frog reading a bright yellow book. Its brilliant aquamarine eyes sat above a powder blue grin. Its reclining torso dotted with gilded spots, "An *alebrije.*"

"Hmm, '*dame un beso*' and now '*alebrije*?' I guess I did teach you a little Spanish over the years. It reminded me of you."

"It's an explosion of whimsy. *Gracias.*"

"You're welcome." She rubbed her hands together. "Aren't you cold?" She glanced into the living room. "Your windows are open."

"Oh, sorry. The movers worked up a sweat. The place smelled like a gym."

She whiffed the air. "Not anymore. How 'bout we close 'em up?"

"Sure. You take the living room, and I'll do the rest." I handed her my literary frog. "Find a worthy place on the mantel for Mr. *Sapo*. Okay?"

She took it, studied it, and wrinkled her brow. "How do you know it's not Ms. Toad?"

"I'm a boy, so is he."

Margo rolled her eyes, shook her head, and turned toward the living room. I heard her mumble something about "Macho."

"I heard that."

"You were meant to."

I scrunched my shoulders.

When I came back, I found her in front of the fireplace, holding the photo of Cisco, DJ, and me.

"Aw, looks like 'Mr. Sapo' is in 'worthy' company."

She'd seen our picture countless times but never let that diminish her tender comments. She placed it back on the mantel and began digging through her purse. "I wanted to wait until I found a frame to show you. But you have to see it." Margo held out a photo of her and I standing at the entrance to UCLA's sculpture garden. "You remember this?"

"Yeah." I gently took the pic and turned it over, expecting a date. "When did we take this?"

"Spring of seventy-one."

"Wow, Margo. You do not age."

She playfully slapped my shoulder. "Oh, stop."

"Can I keep it?" I shot a glance at my pic with Cisco and DJ. "Be a nice contrast to those jokers."

"Without a frame?" She reached for her picture.

I drew back. "I'll get one. Then we can argue about who gets to keep it."

"Alright, for now." She flashed a smile. "Who knows, maybe we'll both end up in the same place it does."

Ignited, I opened my arms. But Margo gripped my shoulders just long enough to lean in and peck my lips. My arms fell. "Was that a down boy?"

She patted my shoulders. "For both of us." Then she glanced about the room. "Ready to unpack? Where should we start?"

I whistled out a cooling breath and stood her photo against mine. "Let's start by filling these bookcases."

She looked the shelves up and down. "It's going to look more like a reading room than a living room. And their bright wood clashes," she turned and pointed at my couch, "against your dark sectional."

I turned shoulder to shoulder with her and said, "Admit it. You've never liked it."

"It's black. Soaks up all the light, don't you think?"

"Okay, I admit that it does seem to dim the place." I internally cringed. I'd bitten her analytical bait.

She slipped her arm around my waist and then rubbed my back. Margo leaned her head against my shoulder. "We've enough light to unpack your heart's baggage, too."

"Uh-uh. I've hemorrhaged enough today."

She turned to meet my gaze. "In what way?"

"The movers wore overalls like Pop's. Had his confidence, too. I kept having to pinch off watery eyes."

"*Mijo*," she began with her maternal tone, "I keep warning you that stuffing your feelings risks having them pop out unexpectedly."

"Hey, been too busy packing for the move to unpack anything else." I stepped away, flopped on the couch, and spread my arms across the back.

"You can run across the room. But you live here now. Never going to be far from my open ears."

I shoveled my hands toward the boxes. "Let's 'open' those instead."

Glaring she said, "Tsk, alright."

By the time Margo and I filled the bookshelves, I had to agree with Floyd. "The mover was right, even unpacked, the place is packed."

"A smaller couch would give ya' more space."

"Can't argue with that. Guess Jumbo has to go."

"Yay! I'll help ya' shop for your new one."

"Deal."

Margo put her hands on her hips. "Well, ready to tackle another room?"

I couldn't risk her stumbling upon Lily's pic, so I patted my belly. "Aren't you hungry? My treat."

"I am, but..." she reached toward the mantel and tapped Mr. Sapo with her manicured nail, "today I'm welcoming you to San Francisco. Dinner is on me."

"But you helped unpack."

"I won't take no for an answer."

"Margo, your generosity is only excelled by your beauty."

She spread her fingers over her heart and patted. "You're making it hard for my steps to be baby ones. We better take two cars."

"Two?"

"Uh-huh. I'm treating you to dinner all the way over at The Cliff House." She leaned back against the fireplace. "If we go in one car, we'll end up here or at my place after, and I'm afraid I won't be able to keep it platonic."

"No?" I said, then sank my voice. "So, what happened to all that 'platonic' restraint you had when you invited me to stay with you before?"

She folded her arms and glanced away, fluttering her long lashes. "That came before my control was tested by our passionate kiss at the door."

I leered and rubbed my hands together. "How about you leave 'control' to me, and we go in my car?"

She bent her arms akimbo. "*Cochino!*"

I stood up, opened my arms, and spread my fingers to flaunt my innocence. "You don't think I can?"

"Nope."

My arms fell along with my gaze, but I looked up and said, "You said we'd be more than *going steady* by the night of the ball. That's only twelve days away."

Margo angled her head, lingering her emerald gaze. "I would like to wait and have our first night together be our crowning event to the Black and White Ball."

Aglow in her gaze, my conscience pricked that I would've felt dirty making love to Margo before extricating Lily's pic. Grateful for the delay to sever Lily's tie, I said, "Then separate cars it should be." I scooped my hand toward the door.

Margo and I found parking near each other and strolled hand in hand into the iconic cliffside restaurant. We scored a window table with its spectacular ocean view.

Upon the arrival of our chilled bottle of sauvignon blanc, we raised our glasses and toasted to "new beginnings."

"The Black and White is coming up fast," she said between oysters on the half shell and our main courses. "You should get in for your tux's final fitting."

"Can we do it together? We'll pick up your dress, too."

She leaned over the linen tablecloth. "*Mijo*, my gown is in my closet, ready to go."

"Oh." I reached across the table, and Margo took my hand. "I'll go tomorrow. Come with me."

"I'm booked solid tomorrow, but call me when you go. On the off chance I've cancellations," Margo squeezed my hand, "I'll join you."

"My phone is due to be installed in the morning. As soon as it's in, I'll make an appointment at the men's shop and call you."

Our waitress arrived with her busboy, who stooped in to clear away our oysters as she unfolded her tray stand.

"Dinner," said Margo.

The waitress courtly served Margo her tilapia and me my sea bass.

Over our meals, Margo excitedly looked forward to the Black and White Ball's performers. Especially to a set by Dinah Shore.

"Dinah Shore?"

"Oh, come on. She's gonna be backed up by an old-school orchestra. We can dance the boogie-woogie like our parents."

"Didn't I embarrass myself enough at La Peña?"

"You were fine. Besides, she sings early. Then we can take in the likes of Lady Bianca, Tito Puente—"

"What, no Santana?" I puffed my chest and crossed my arms.

She poked her empty fork at me. "Pete Escovedo's performing. He's played with Carlos."

I shrank into my seat. "Alright. I guess I'll still go."

Margo glared back. "If you don't. No dessert."

I perked up. "I'm going, I'm going."

We topped off dinner with a tiramisu made even more delicious by feeding each other from the tips of our long dessert spoons. I patted my stomach after she fed me the last fluffy bite. "I'm not used to being indulged like this. And thanks for suspending the psychobabble."

"You're welcome. But I did sneak a little into your apartment earlier."

Despite her playful lilt, I reluctantly asked, "You did?"

She squinted above a crooked grin. "What'd you do with Mr. Sapo's gift bag."

"Left it in my bedroom. Why?"

"Remember its and the tissue paper's colors?"

I cocked my head. "Gold and red, right?"

"'Right.' That was a successive approximation."

"A what?"

"A nudge away from your LA allegiances."

"Okay, I give. What do you mean?"

"Red and gold are the Forty-Niners' colors."

I grabbed my forehead. "Ah. I get it. No more rooting for the Rams."

She rocked her head. "See. You've approximated a local."

87

I snorted my resignation.

Despite arriving in separate cars, Margo did let me drive us the short distance to the Sunset Lounge for nightcaps.

With no empty stools at the bar, we settled for a cramped two-chair table against the back wall. Our knees bumped before we shuffled our thighs together. "Is this alright, *mijo*?"

"I'm with you. Couldn't be better." Margo smiled, and I added, "Makes me want to pinch myself."

She cocked her head. "We have a ways to go to boost that confidence of yours, don't we? Should I put on my clinical cap?" She glanced around, patting her pockets. "Where'd I put it?"

I yanked the backs of my hands to my shoulders, fingers splayed. "No, no. That's okay." From the corner of my eye, I saw a waitress heading our way. "Ready to order?"

After the waitress returned with Margo's chardonnay and my cab, we toasted the Sunset Lounge and christened it "Our Place."

I leaned in, eager to shrink the space between us. "You know, Margo, if it wasn't for your light, I'd be stuck forever in that black hole in my living room."

Margo reached under the table and patted my knee. "You're giving me too much credit, but it'll be fun helping you pick a new sofa."

She sat back and thoughtfully bounced her chin upon tented fingertips. After suggesting a litany of colors, styles, and fabrics, she must've recognized my dazed look. "Or, we can check out what they have at the Price Club warehouse."

"I don't qualify for membership."

"I'll put you on mine." Margo leaned across the table and, in a conspiratorial whisper, said, "If I'm tied up and you have time to see what they have before I can add you to my membership, find a solo member going in and stroll in next to her. Couples only flash one card. You won't be able to buy anything, but you can look around."

"Didn't know you were so slick."

She leaned back and smirked. "Getting through obstacles is what therapists do." Without another word, she reached for her glass and, with a glance, invited me to do the same. We clinked them together. Then I dug change out of my pocket and spread it in my palm.

"What are you doing?"

I met her quizzical glare. "Need quarters for the jukebox."

"Watcha gonna play?"

"Think they have Herman's Hermits?"

"'Herman's Hermits?'"

"Yeah, I want to hear, 'I'm Into Something Good.'"

She grinned, shook her head, and then looked off into the distance. "Was I even in sixth grade when that came out?" Then she waived me off. "Go on."

The opening thumps of "In-A-Gadda-Da-Vida" followed me back to our table.

"What the?" Margo's face twisted into a question mark.

"Not mine. I picked 'Stuck on You.'"

"Lionel Richie—sweet. No Hermits, huh?"

I poked the air between us. "Bingo."

After Lionel's sweet serenade, I tried talking her into another chardonnay, but her busy schedule made her call it a night. "I guess, if I have to, I'll drive you back to the Cliff House."

Back at her car, she gave me a luscious kiss goodnight that came with a complete body snuggle. I reluctantly withdrew as Margo drew her hands from my around my neck. "It's getting harder to let you go," I said.

Margo's fingers found mine, and she laced them together. "I'm counting on that, scaredy-cat."

"Oh sure, throw that in my face."

Margo slipped behind the wheel of her car, and we kissed again through her window. "Talk to you tomorrow."

I watched her drive away, but still simmering, I stopped outside my sedan to take in the rolling Pacific. The crisp ocean breeze made my skin bumpy but couldn't douse my internal glow. I inhaled the rhythmic surf's clean breath, fresh as my new start.

Eleven

I recalled Margo's moist lips upon mine as sleep faded from my first morning in the city. I snuggled into my pillow, but the sun's pesky rays bled through the mini blinds and lit my face. My eyes popped open. I whipped my back to the window only to face a stack of boxes and the charge of which one hid Lily's book? "Humph."

I'd get no rest ignoring her. After a quick shower and a careful shave, I tromped back to my bedroom, where I slipped into comfortable jeans and a faded UCLA sweatshirt. I began slicing open boxes and putting away clothes. In a battered box of shirts, I found my crushed answering machine. A casualty of the move.

"Finally." I lifted *The Tale of Kiều* from its sweatered hideout. I'd get it in the mail but couldn't resist another peek at Lily. I slid out her picture and sat Kiều on my nightstand beside my planner. Lily's timid gaze reminded me that it had been captured before survival had plundered her innocence. Then, it hit me that my defiant smirk on the mantel was caught before Mai's death. I had to compare our innocent pics. I rushed into my living room. But when I ushered Lily next to me, DJ, and Cisco, I winced at the guilty clash between Lily's and Margo's identically cropped photos. I tipped Margo's snapshot face down.

Staring into me and Lily's creaseless teenage faces amped our kindred tie. My heart jumped, threatening my balance. I grabbed the mantel's ledge, knocking her pic to the floor. I picked her up and slid her face down next to Margo's photo. Stretching my arms against the mantel, I dropped my head between my elbows. Between pumping my arms and my pounding pulse, the doorbell chimed in. I snatched Lily's photo, denied myself a look, and slid it into my back pocket.

"Pac Bell," said the young tech holding his tool kit in one hand and a thick phone book in the other.

"Come in," I said, welcoming the distraction.

"How many phones you want and where?" He handed me the directory and casually glanced around.

"One. On the nightstand in the bedroom." I'd decided that the compact place didn't need more than that. I showed him into my room, tossed the directory upon my bed, then took *The Tale of Kiều* off my nightstand. I pulled Lily's pic out of my pocket without suffering a last peek and nestled it between Kiều's pages. Then, I grabbed my planner for Lily's address.

Marching to my Zippo's tempo into the kitchen, I wrestled with what to write to Lily. *Thank you, Cisco* was all my dense deliberation came up with. I ripped open the box, dominating my small table, and rummaged around until I found the scissors. I cut off the box's cardboard flaps and trimmed them into a protective cover for Kiều.

I wrote my pithy thanks and folded the note tightly before slipping it behind the book's cover. While wrapping Kiều, I managed to think up a bogus post office box for a return address. As I penned Lily's zip code, the phone man popped into the kitchen. "All done."

He gave me my new number and reminded me it was printed on the phone.

I thanked him, walked him out, and returned to the kitchen to inspect Lily's carefully bound parcel. Smoothing down the blisters on the packaging tape, I told myself that Kiều's imminent departure removed Lily from between Margo and me. I took it with me to my bedroom and called the tailor. He gave me a midafternoon appointment. I called Margo.

"Good mornin'. Ya' callin' from your new number?"

"I am." I recited it a digit at a time to let her jot it down.

"What time ya' goin' to the tailor's?"

I told her and asked if she'd meet me?

"Can't tell. No cancellations yet. Go get fitted, and I'll meet ya' there if I can. If not, how 'bout I drop by your place around five to help ya' with the rest of your boxes?"

"Sounds good." Imagining Lily behind me, I floated upon Margo's buoyant lilt and sailed into a bold offer. "How about I make you a key to my apartment?"

"That's quite a stride for a baby step." Then she crested her voice, "How 'bout I match your daring with a trade? I'll bring ya' one of mine, too."

My breath swooped in. "Really?"

"Don't be so surprised," she said airily.

Aloft after our call and anxious to find a place to cut a key, I flipped through the Yellow Pages and found a hardware store. Then I slipped out of my sweatshirt and into a tan polo, layered with a gray wool sweater, and grabbed Kiều. I bounded out my door.

With Kiều in the mail and a key for Margo in my pocket, I strolled Noe's shops in search of a key ring worthy of Margo. Satisfied with my braided leather find with its turquoise pendant, my grumbling belly led me into an immaculate, airy cafe. Their tasty *huevos rancheros* convinced me that I'd discovered a place that'd satisfy Margo, too.

I tipped the waitress and glanced at my watch. The day was slipping by. I strode to my car and headed downtown.

The tailor pinned, measured and chalked as I stood before the mirrors. He confidently promised he'd complete the alterations by the next day. Asked if I could return at the same time tomorrow? I agreed, glad the CFO had granted me a flexible schedule to settle in. However, now I faced traffic that threatened to strand Margo on the sidewalk before I got home.

Stretching my legs the block and a half to my apartment, I turned down my street and recognized Margo's lithe steps coming from the opposite direction. I shot up my wave, relieved I hadn't kept her waiting.

"What timing," she said as we met in front of my place. She rewarded me with a passionate body hug and wet kiss.

Sparkling from our embrace, I dangled her key between us.

She cupped it. "I love it." Then she reached into her purse and brought out a leather-laced key of her own. "Great minds think alike."

We exchanged keys, then I bowed and scooped my hand toward the stairs. "After you. Try it out."

After a slight curtsy, she bounded up the steps.

I followed her in and closed the door behind me as she walked into the living room. Then I heard, "Who's she?"

I rushed in to see Margo holding Lily's photo straight out between us. I'd mailed the wrong pic.

"I—I found it unpacking."

"'It?'"

Her familiar feminist glower rebuked my dismissive *it* as I lurched into another lie. "She cleaned our hooch. Lots of GIs hired locals for that."

"Bobby mentioned that." She turned Lily around for a look. "I don't remember seeing *her* in your old photo album." Her curious tone came without accusation. The old photo hadn't aroused suspicion.

"I'd misplaced it. Didn't make it in."

Margo glanced at the mantel and then back at me. "Where's our picture?"

"Dropped it off for a custom frame." Another lie hammered into my ledger of deceit.

"That'll cost you."

I flinched, but she'd turned to prop Lily's photo against mine.

"Old photos can pry up buried memories." Margo faced me but listed against the mantel. "What made you put her picture by yours?"

I dodged her eyes. Battling my conscience and its risk to our romance, I slinked over to my couch, sat, and muttered a splinter of truth. "I guess I wanted to compare her smooth face to mine at that age."

Margo crossed her arms and squeezed her shoulders. "Maybe you displayed her to remind us both to stop ignoring Vietnam."

Her grip braced her for Nam. I could save her from the war with the truth about Lily. But it would wreck us.

Margo bit her bottom lip and said, "How about you start by telling me her name."

I cleared my throat to gasp, "Lily."

"'Lily' took the wind out of you." Her eyes didn't leave my face, but then she squinted. "Was she your girlfriend?"

"No—never. Just another desperate kid trying to survive like the rest of us."

"But *her* picture is on your mantel."

I pressed my palms onto my knees, locked my elbows, and straightened my back to summon my confession. "Ah…"

Margo's hands lost their grip and slid from her drooping shoulders. "Les…was Lily killed?"

Her grief brokered a place to hide my madam. A *yes* could conceal her—but that lie struck Mai's tomb. I'd be burying Lily like I'd tried to do with Mai. A kink in my gut yanked my hand to my belly. I couldn't shovel dirt on either one of them. I whimpered, "No, not her."

"'Not her?'" Then her chin sank toward her rising chest as she fluttered in a breath. "I know how painful this is. But Lily's appearance, like your GI slang, is saying you can't hide anymore from the *her* you did lose in Vietnam."

Margo came over and eased down next to me. She glanced toward Lily's pic. "Did Lily know her?"

Her question rolled invitingly off her tongue but didn't ease my knotted belly. "No," I droned as my knots dissolved into nausea before Mai's looming ghost. Tenting my arms upon my thighs, I buried my face into my palms and swallowed hard to moisten my throat. "She—she didn't know Linh Mai."

"'Linh Mai.'" Margo rested her hand between my shoulder blades. "Tell me about Linh Mai."

Tears seeped in with the specter of my little girl. "She's my...my little girl."

Margo's voice quaked. "You lost a daughter."

Her pain sapped my tears but set off ringing in my ears. I straightened up, scraped the moisture from my cheeks, and turned to her. "No, no—Linh Mai was an orphan."

Margo's eyes had fogged over. She leaned back and reached into her purse. She teased out a couple of tissues. She offered me one as she dabbed her eyes. I declined, palm out, and slouched back into the cushion.

"*Mijo*, how old was your little girl?" Her measured lilt left no doubt about her acceptance of Mai as my little girl.

Margo's affirmation rippled through me like a warm welcome to Mai and soothed my queasy belly. "Seven or eight. The orphanage nuns weren't sure."

"How'd you meet?" Her voice's tender sway harkened Mai's sunny spirit. Like when Lily'd reached kinder memories—I stiffened against Lily's reach.

"You need to stop, *mijo*?" Margo patted my thigh, then squeezed my knee.

"No. I'm okay," I said, though I felt that's what she'd prefer.

"I'd ridden shotgun for the medics to Mai's orphanage. While they gave inoculations and provided first aid, I crouched near the gate and watched the tree line." Mai's mischievous grin materialized between me and the fireplace.

"The little munchkin snuck up behind me and poked my shoulder. I shot up and spun around, but she'd jumped back, giggling and hopping from one foot to another, pointing and shouting, *You're it. You're it*." Tapping that day's ancient memory rekindled Mai's innocent warmth. A flurry of her contagious laughter canceled the ringing between my ears.

"Oh, she spoke English."

"A little. Other GIs had gone there and played with the kids."

Margo focused her soft gaze upon my profile. "Linh Mai sounds adorable."

"More than that. You wouldn't believe the little firecracker's spunk. After that day, I volunteered every chance I got to guard the medics on their visits there. Then I began dragging DJ and Cisco along to watch the perimeter so I could play tag with her and the other kids." Picturing myself kicking up dust in my pursuit of Mai and a gaggle of other goofballs brought back the glee of their boisterous laughter. I chuckled at that silly memory.

"I'd bring the orphanage food, toys, other donations." Mai's diaphanous image ran toward me with open arms. "And always a special treat for Mai." I inhaled a chaste breath and felt the sparkle of Mai's indomitable spirit as if she'd flung herself into my arms again.

I stretched my arm atop the back cushion behind Margo. "Mai erased all the war's ugliness."

"*Mijo*, do you know you're grinning?"

"I guess I am, huh." I slightly bobbed my head.

"Your lighter's quiet, too."

I gaped and then shook my head. "It is. Isn't it?"

"Remember I called your lighter your talisman? Said its harmless clicks reminded you of your harmless nature. I believe Mai touched your loving nature. Still does, judging by that smile."

Margo's charitable insight fit pleasantly with Mai's sweet visitation. But grief's tug reminded me that I owed them both the truth about her death. I averted my eyes.

"Mijo?"

"Margo, I only had to survive Nam a year. But Mai would always be an orphan and would've had to endure that fucking war after I'd gone."

I glanced into Margo's stiff gaze. She'd braced for Mai's death. I bent forward and clutched my face. "She died because of me." Tears bled between my fingers.

"You?" Margo's voice disintegrated as I plummeted back to the day I rocked a gutted Mai in my arms. I smelled the metal of Mai's bleed and felt her blood throb between my fingers. Her body trembled against mine until her last rattled breath.

"Mijo—Les," a distant voice insisted the second time. I felt an arm stretch across my shoulders and pull me away from Mai. I scowled at my hands wet with tears, not blood?

Blinking through Mai's bloody apparition, I recognized my blurry living room. I'd gotten Mai killed long ago. Grief had aborted time.

"What made you," Margo's voice cracked before she added, "say that?"

I met Margo's watery stare. Her words had broken, unable to ask how I'd killed Mai. Still, she slid her warm hand between my shoulders and caressed my back.

I looked away but sputtered through my sodden throat. "I—I made the medics drive us to her orphanage." I plowed my face through my hands but couldn't push back my tears.

"You, DJ, and Cisco?"

"Almost got them killed, too." Airing their peril sapped my lungs. I gulped another breath. "The VC opened up on us outside the gate." Then I rasped between shuddering sobs, "Mai got hit running to me."

Margo's fingers left my back. I turned to see her breath quake as she patted tissue against her tears. She'd buckled under Mai's murder. But she returned her caress as her dewy gaze met mine. "*Mijo*, you mustn't let my tears stop you."

She didn't know the horror she'd invited. I censored Mai's fate into words no more gruesome than *ambush* and *stray bullet*. Cruel terms sanitized into rank euphemisms by every bloodless, black-and-white cowboy movie ever fed to a baby boomer.

I strained against my tears. "Charlie's bullet was meant for me. Not Mai."

"*Mijo*, you're not responsible for things you can't control." She punctuated her plea with a gentle hug.

I rubbed my damp cheeks. "DJ said the same thing. But that's not how I feel."

"Do you 'feel' Mai blames you?"

"Why wouldn't she?" I said against my suddenly taut jaw.

Her hand closed around her tissue as she rested it upon her knee. "Would you blame her if she had been you?"

"Of course not," I snapped, burning back my tears. "Not her faul—" my tongue collapsed against the contradiction.

"Right, so how could she blame you?"

A flutter of exoneration fanned my conscience but withered against my sense of betrayal. "Don't I owe her?"

"What would Linh Mai say you 'owe her,' *mijo*?"

I jerked a shrug to emphasize the obvious. "To never kill anybody else."

Margo clutched her throat. "Oh my God—that's it."

"Wha—what?" My face pinched.

"You believe your love is deadly."

I leered through a flash of Margo's cadaverous face. "Making you cry is just a start."

She softened her gaze. "M*ijo*, I cry because I care about you and feel your pain. Not because you wounded me."

"What's the difference?" I said, unable to cool my glare.

"'The difference' is that your love didn't harm me."

"It's still my fault."

Margo tilted her head. "You're defending misplaced guilt."

"'Misplaced?' If it wasn't for me, Mai'd be alive." Fidgeting, I shot my gaze about the living room to keep from spouting, *If I hadn't hurt Jessica, she'd be sitting here, not you.*

"*Mijo*, I think Mai's loss tore open the wound left by your mother's abandonment. It convinced you that your love is fatal."

"I told you, Pop and I made Mom miserable—chased her away."

"How are you to blame?"

The night Mom bolted spun across my brain like a loose reel. My shoulders hooked forward. "She rushed out the door, glared at me over her shoulder, and spat that because of me she *had* to marry Pop." I evaded Margo's sympathetic gaze. An easy task through that dark memory peppering the light.

"What I'm hearing is she'd tried to do the right thing by marrying your pop. But she felt trapped. That breeds resentment, anger. They must've boiled over when you blocked her escape. She took her spite out on you."

Her shift in blame flickered like a distant light. "Not my fault?"

"Not even close. Les, first, she made her misery your fault. Then she charged out the door making your love and loss parts of the same wound. Left you primed to answer for the bullet that took Mai."

Margo's exonerating wedge blunted against my liability for Jessica's pain. "Jessica's tears were nobody's fault but mine."

She scooted to the edge of the seat and brought her face to bear upon mine. "I was back here when you moved in with her. All you ever said was that it didn't work out. What happened?"

Glancing at her from the corners of my eyes, I said, "Things were fine until she told me I'd make a good father."

"In what way did that change things?"

Hadn't she been listening? I cocked my head. "Whose stricken face just tore me up?"

She lingered her gaze as if to let my irritation cool. "You broke up with a woman you loved to escape Mai's unbearable loss."

Margo'd reached the same conclusion I'd run into at Lily's Spa. "I know that now. Didn't then." I rubbed my clammy palms together. "Fooled myself into believing I was still too young for kids."

"So, since Jessica, you've withheld your love to protect yourself from further heartbreak."

"And everybody else, too."

"You believe Jessica was a casualty of your love. I would argue that your love was a fatality of misplaced guilt over your mother's desertion. If I'm wrong, then you don't love me. After all, you've never hurt me."

I felt the salve of our injury-free years. Still, I sputtered, "I—I've loved you since the day we met."

She leaned back, tucked her legs beneath her, and patted the back cushion. "Come here, *mijo*."

I sat back, lured by the prospect of acquittal. "It's hard to see it your way after all this time."

"What 'way' is that?"

I hissed out my nose. "You're going to make me say it, aren't you?"

"Say what?"

I clenched my jaw. "That maybe my love isn't fatal."

"And if not. Then?"

"'Then,' maybe I'm not guilty for what happened to Mom and Mai." But Margo's light against that darkness lit a warning. "What'll happen without guilt's restraint?"

Leading with a knowing grin, she reached into her purse, pulled out my key, and dangled it between us. "See? It's already happened. Anybody hurt?"

I winced at my bungled break with Lily. "Not yet."

She dropped my key into her purse. "In time, you'll see that lowering guilt's guard hasn't injured either one of us."

My heart's lurch to believe her snagged on my lingering tie to Lily. Tripped an urge to tell her the truth about my madam. But I cowered at that risk. Instead, I tried to appease my conscience with another admission. "Then I should warn you about my ugly scars, too."

She tilted her head.

"I've burn scars on my back."

"Still trying to scare me off?"

I heaved a heavy breath. "Suppose I am, huh?"

"They've poked against my hugs since UCLA. Came home with you from the war, didn't they?"

I darted my eyes between my knees and Margo's. "You felt them."

"And I'm still here. Encouraged even more by your bold openness today."

"'Bold?' Raw is more like it."

"Give yourself credit. You opened your wounds despite fear they'd chase me away."

I cast my gaze about the room. "Your scalpel *mentis* didn't leave me much choice." Then I shifted into a beleaguered nod. "Don't think I can take anymore."

Margo stroked my shoulder. "You've earned a break."

I watched her glance about the room. "Let's find some boxes to unpack," she said.

I raised my hands. "Thought I unloaded enough."

She elbowed me playfully. "Cute. Just talkin' about boxes."

"Cool. All that's left are in the kitchen."

Twelve

"*The cloak and dagger dangles, Madams light the candles, In ceremonies of the horsemen, Even a pawn must hold a grudge—*" I flopped over and slapped the snooze button. Damn, reminded by Dylan I'd sent Lily Margo's pic. Bad enough, I had to work this morning. Should've set my alarm to a jazz station. I switched it off.

I swung my feet to the floor and squeezed my knees. Lily'd get Kiều tomorrow or Friday. Then I'd have to slosh through embarrassment to face her and trade photos. A stolen time between work and evenings with Margo. I lumbered into the living room to vacate Lily's picture from the mantel. I grabbed a book off a bookshelf.

Back in my bedroom, I forced my lingering stare away from shy Lily and hid her picture between the pages of *The Devil's Dictionary*—a fitting hideout. I stashed it in my closet.

In my sliver of a bathroom, I splashed cold water on my face, wondering what I'd tell Margo when Lily's photo disappeared. Without an answer, I toweled my cheeks and pondered the lucky guy in the mirror who'd dine with Margo tonight. Dared to hope my deceptions could hide Lily until she was gone.

The CFO intercepted me as I opened my office door, signaling he had a surprise for me. "Les, can you come with me to

LA? I have to meet with the buyers of our old building in the morning. They need some hand-holding over operating costs."

Though my short-notice travel demands were nothing new to Margo, it'd disappoint me to miss our date tonight. And I was supposed to pick up my tux this afternoon. "When do we leave?"

"Fly out tonight. That work for you?"

"No problem. How long will we be gone?" I said, relieved I had time to get to the tailor's.

He rubbed his chin. "Should be back Friday."

"Meet at SFO?"

"Sure." He walked off. His custom when done.

At my desk, I fired up my computer to review our old building's operational costs and reached for the phone to call Margo. Our travel service's call interrupted. Given an itinerary that'd get us home late Friday afternoon, I imagined Lily'd have Kiều by then. That cracked open a chance to put Lily behind me with no more than a final fib to Margo. I could tell her I'd be back too late Friday to see her. See Lily instead, to trade pics. I'd call Lily as soon as I got home on Friday.

I tongued the inside of my mouth and phoned Margo. Told her that I had to fly to LA tonight with the CFO. That I wouldn't be back till late Friday, adding that she should make plans without me.

"Guess I'll have to wait until the weekend to make sure you get rid of that couch of yours," she said and then giggled.

I chuckled to belie my guilty conscience.

Thirteen

The CFO let me drive the rental to visit my father's grave while he wrapped up Friday's final meet. Sniveling over Pop's tomb, I reminded him of the girl with the impressive *peepers*. Recalled his rise from the kitchen table to shake Margo's hand. "You know, the one you said, *Don't let that one getaway.*" Chuckling, I patted his headstone. "Not going to, Pop. Wish you were here to see her again." I caressed his marker and whispered, "Miss you."

I'd rubbed away my tears by the time I picked up my boss. Our recap of the trip's success helped distract me from leaving Pop behind. Then, at LAX, our on-time ETA to SFO kindled my plan to see Lily.

I'd taken public transportation to SFO to apply one of Margo's prescriptions toward becoming a local. But my boss had left his beemer in long-term parking. I took him up on his offer to drive me home.

I called Lily's from my bedroom.

"Lily's Spa."

I didn't recognize her pleasant lilt. "Lily, please."

"She's not here. But come. I'll take just as good care of you."

Did Lily do customers? That wasn't the impression she'd left me. "Is she coming back?"

"Didn't say."

"Can I leave a message?"

"No pen. Wait."

I heard clomping around and then some shuffling. Enough time to realize that leaving Lily my number did the opposite of severing our tie. "Never mind, I'll call back."

"Okay."

I clunked the phone into its cradle. I'd try again later.

My rumbling belly interrupted my dig for my Zippo. I plodded into the kitchen, swung open the frig only to be reminded I'd eaten my last slice of pizza. No milk either, but not in the mood for Cheerios anyway, I opened the cupboard to my can of menudo. Puckering my lips, I decided to save it for a hangover. I'd eat out.

I called Lily's before I left with the same result. Considered calling Margo but decided to keep trying the spa. In the meantime, I thought, what the hell, I'll extend my hunger as penance for ducking Margo and indulge her complaint against my sectional. I'd sneak into the Price Club to peruse their furniture and then grab a burrito on the way home. Wolf it down before trying Lily, yet again.

Neither Price Club's door monitor nor the woman next to me pushing her cart glanced at me twice as I strolled in. I doubted I'd run into Margo here on a Friday night, but merging into the crowd provided a comfortable anonymity. I snorted. Why hide? It'd be one less omission to track. If I ran into her, I could tell her we'd unexpectedly wrapped up early. That I didn't want to interrupt her Friday night, so I took up her scheme to sneak into the Price Club. Of course she'd challenge me on that, then she'd accept that my struggling confidence had reared its unentitled head. I rubbed my shoulders and strode over to their furniture display at the center of their discount ballroom.

Beige fabric made the only difference between their huge sectional and mine. But next to it sat an identically upholstered compact couch that looked good enough for me. I cupped my elbow and scratched my chin. Would it pass Margo's taste test? I'd come back with her to find out. I decided to tour the place.

Must've been hunger that lured me toward their freezers. I scanned the glass doors for microwavable delights. Spotting generous variety packs of burritos, once I became a member I'd bulk up here. I patted my grumbling belly. It didn't appreciate the tease.

"Hello Cisco," melodically floated up from behind. Lily's reflection crystalized upon the freezer's glass door.

Flat-footed, I didn't have her photo with me and really didn't know if she'd gotten Margo's yet.

I gulped and then turned to face her. "Lily, hi." Though taken by her beauty, replete in her smart, black business suit, my paranoia spiked. I eyed behind her for Margo.

Lily glanced over her shoulder. "Who der?"

I shook my head as much to shed my jitters as to embellish their excuse. "Thought I saw a friend." My reduction of Margo to friend stabbed back, but I jerked my head toward the squealing wheel of a cart. The man I'd seen at her spa rolled up a flatbed stacked with white towels and jugs of mouthwash. *Where's the grab bag of condoms?* cracked across my promiscuous brain.

He didn't acknowledge me, and after their brief exchange in Vietnamese, he squeaked away, glancing back at me.

"Who's that?" I asked.

"Brother." I registered her fluently pronounced *brother* before she added, "I get book today. It have picture of you with pretty girl."

I brought my fist to my mouth and coughed through the sludge. "I just moved here Monday. While unpacking, I mixed up your picture with a friend's—my best friend's—in my rush to return your book," I said, feeling slimy for reducing Margo to *best friend*.

"My 'picture?'"

"Ah, yeah. Found a photo of you in your book. You're standing in front of a hooch."

Clasping her chest, she glanced away, resembling more the innocent teen in her photo than a madam. Following a meek smile, her eyes searched mine. "You say friend picture. Not you wife?"

That appealing glimpse of her lost innocence blanched Margo from my reply. "I told you that I'm not married."

"I believe when you take book. But when I get picture in mail, I think you move here with wife and can't come see me."

Can't? I let that contraction, along with her articulate *brother,* distract me from my snub of Margo. "I live alone," I said and caught the glare of a couple with a crammed cart in back of us. "I think somebody needs a bag of burritos." Lily and I padded to the center of the aisle. Families pushing bulging carts flowed around us.

"Where she live?"

Rapt in her interest, I'd discourage her by admitting her competition lived in SF—*competition?*   I strained against my fickle lapse. "Ahem. Here, San Francisco."

Lily's amber eyes found mine. "You like *my* picture?"

"I do," I guiltily admitted.

"You like, you keep."   She put her arm through mine and led me to a quieter aisle among brightly packaged laundry detergents.

Lily'd rescued me from having to explain to Margo what happened to her photo. Her lumpy sofa crested upon a wave of gratitude. "Hey, you want my couch?"

"Why you no want?"

Her caution asserted the impulsivity of my offer. "Ah, it's too big for my little apartment."

"Must see first."

I stumbled back, glancing around for Margo. "When?"

She looked at me up and down. "Tonight. You say no wife home."

Margo had a key. Could she be there decorating? But my throat seized against forsaking my offer. Then, my conscience clamored for punishment. I dropped my arms and flopped open my hands. "Come see for yourself," I said to expose myself to the justice of getting caught by both women.

Lily threaded her arm back through mine to lead us out of laundry land and toward my guilty surrender to fate.

Moping along, mitigative thoughts penetrated my gloom. Surely, confronting Margo with Lily would cost us our romance. But my deceit wasn't aimed at fucking her, like *Dr. Mentiroso's*.

Could blowing it before I slept with her leave room for her forgiveness? Save our friendship? And like my old sergeant said about working girls, *Them girls ain't gonna give ya' their real names. They need a shield to keep their whoring outta the rest of their lives.* Lily'd understand my duplicity. Maybe enough to leave room for me in her life. Running into Margo felt slightly less fatal. I forced my feet up from their gallows shuffle.

"Where you live, Cisco?"

"Noe Valley," I said as she traded greetings with an attractive middle-aged woman, also tastefully dressed in black.

After she passed, I asked, "A friend of yours?"

"Rose? She own place I work before I open my spa."

"What's with the black? Some sorta madam's dress code?" I quipped to lift my mood.

Lily slowed our pace, and I saw the light in her eyes flicker. "All madams wear black. There's darkness in our hearts." Then she glanced up at me, adding, "Like yours, Cisco."

I felt her scarred assertion of our blighted pasts—in grammatically correct English.

She resumed her stride, and I kept up. "We find brudder. Finish, follow you home." Her double *d* thumped back. She deliberately mangled her English. But before I could accuse her, she pointed across my chest. "You look there for brudder." Then she pointed left. "I look here."

The squawk of a wheel closing from behind made me look back. *Brudder* had tracked us. Had he been a Kit Carson scout in Nam?

Judging by the disinfectants and paper towels added to their cart, he'd been gathering cleaning supplies. After their flutter of

Vietnamese, he stepped to the front of the flatbed and extended his hand.

"Cisco, *Bảo*," Lily said.

"Cisco." Impressed by his firm grip, I saw a deliberating juror behind his poker gaze.

He returned a skeptical grunt, then stepped back to steer their cart. He pushed ahead, but instead of coursing toward checkout, he made a left between toys and books.

Lily slowed to browse a selection of children's titles. Of course, she read English. But I lagged by their cart, stuck at reconciling bordello antiseptics with children's bedtime stories.

She called me over without looking away from her selection to ask my opinion of Dr. Seuss.

Stumbling over her contradictions, I fumbled out that my parents never introduced me to Dr. Seuss.

Lily paged through, snickered, and said, "Mine didn't either."

"Right, Seuss isn't Vietnamese." But I latched on to her, *didn't.* "You speak better English than you let on."

"You pay attention." She didn't look up.

"So, why the broken English?"

She dipped her chin. "It's easy to refuse a customer his sick fantasy with *Me no understand.*"

Did she mean when she did johns or when they asked for something twisted from one of her masseuses? Damn—jealousy!

She handed me *The Cat in the Hat.*

I took the book, and Mai's image glanced between us. "Uh, I'm thinking a youngster would like it. Who's it for?"

She slid the book out of my hands and handed it to Bảo. Her eyes didn't leave my face. "Daughter, Annie. Now you know I am a mother, too. All you told me is that you're a CPA. You have children?"

"No kids. Never married." *And Cisco's not my name* about popped out of my mouth, but I shook my head instead.

Lily shifted her gaze to the spine of another book. "Maybe after I see your house, someday you see mine." She picked up the title and offered the cover for my opinion. She bumped her shoulder into mine. "What do you think?"

I endorsed the book but ignored seeing her house. It's Margo's door I should've longed to enter, not hers. Lily didn't pursue the omission. Margo wouldn't've let me get away with that.

A stack of titles and various toys made it onto their cart. I couldn't imagine they were all for Annie. But I didn't ask whose children she was spoiling for fear of losing my grip on Mai's memory. It came as a relief when Bảo resumed his role as consumer point man and led us to checkout.

In the parking garage, I helped Bảo load Lily's mommy van. Then Lily and I drove off together with Bảo in tow.

She heard my belly rumble, and I told her I don't eat much. Hid I'd lost my appetite in dread of running into Margo. I squeezed the steering wheel and changed the subject. "You let me read about Kiều. What happened to her happened to you, didn't it?"

She looked away and stared out the windshield. "If I tell you, you must tell me why you come to my spa."

"That's fair," I said, intent on disclosing little more than I frequented places like hers because no one gets hurt.

"I told you I am not in this business in my country." Lily paused and her eyes fluttered before she went on. "But if you don't give men what they want, they take it anyway. Government man beat me, took my flower when I was young." Her body deflated as her eyes wandered into the distance.

I imagined her seeing the plow of her rapist's punches. But when I patted her arm to comfort her, she jerked back and wedged against the door.

I yanked back my open fingers. "Sorry—sorry."

She blinked at my hand as if expecting a fist and grabbed her shoulders. "He told my father the government take his land if he tell police. My father send me away to live with uncle."

"That's harsh." But even as I said it, my words bled anemic before the gravity of her rape. Her neutral glance confirmed my sympathetic flop.

She continued at a frosty clip that could've been her way to suffer going on. "Too young to know better, I think if I come to America, things be different. My friend clean hooches and introduce me to my American husband. He a lifer, so when I leave Vietnam, we live at Schofield Army base in Hawaii." Lily paused to breathe.

Clumsy around her wounds, I gingerly repeated what she'd told me at her spa. "You said he ended up liking someone else."

She dislodged herself from the door and leaned back against the seat. "Before I catch him with his girlfriend, he said we need money, so I must go to work. But my English was not good. He find me a job hustling drinks in a hostess bar." She snickered. "Same place he went when he say he had night duty."

He'd set her on Kiều's path. I slouched in my seat and said, "I'm sorry, Lily."

She glanced down and massaged her knees. "I met Rose there. She told me I could meet men after work for more money, like her. When I said no, she say, *They take our respect anyway, make them pay for it.* But we stay in touch when she come to San Francisco to open her massage parlor." Lily breathed out, knitted her brow, and folded her arms.

Had she said enough? I grappled with whether or not to ask, but she asked me, "What secrets bring you to my place?"

Witnessing her pain, I desperately wanted her to know I wasn't like her ex. "I don't hurt anyone at places like yours."

Lilly twisted to see Bảo behind us. "You hit women?" she spat.

I groaned, "No—never."

"You fuck other woman in your girlfriend's bed?"

Though I hadn't, being unfaithful to Jessica, deflated that detail into a murmur. "I never did that."

She straightened into her seat. "My husband hit me when I catch him in *my* bed with his girlfriend."

Squirming behind the wheel, I added, "What I mean is nobody's feelings get hurt. After breaking my girlfriend's heart years ago, I stopped dating. Started going to places like yours instead."

Lily squinted. "Why break her heart?"

I couldn't relive Mai's death. So I told her what I told myself at the time. "We lived together. But when she said we should have a kid, I didn't want to. She made me leave."

"Did you love her?"

My voice dipped. "Yeah—Yes. I did."

"Why not have a baby?"

"I wasn't ready. Too young." I evaded her gaze.

"You're older now, but still come to my spa. What are you afraid of?"

My lungs flagged, but I invoked what Margo contested. "Everybody I love gets hurt."

"How?" she said, her squint quizzical, guarded.

Hobbling away from Mai's tomb, I told Lily that I drove my mother away. When I told her how old I was, she dismissed my hurting Mom with a precision foreign to me. "Only when children *get* hurt can they hurt mother." Still, I confessed that I'd neglected my father up to the moment he died. But when she heard my voice crack at witnessing Pop whither away, she said, "Too hard to watch."

Lily rested her elbow on the armrest. "Cisco, you're not to blame for those things."

Nearing my apartment and maybe closing on Margo, I saw no room for acquittal. Glancing between Lily and the road ahead, I said, "I wish."

As I pulled in front of my dark apartment, a spark of relief at no sign of Margo drowned in a swell of alarm that she'd still drop by. I let Bảo park in the rare space at my front door and dropped Lily off while I went searching for a parking spot. The block behind my street offered a vacant space. I locked my car and grabbed my Zippo.

To keep my stride, I told myself that no way Margo'd show up unannounced—but I'd told her I'd be back late. She'd no reason to call first. Click, click. My feet slowed, but I turned the corner to my street and could see Lily talking to Bảo half a block away.

Trading my lighter for my keys, I forced a casual stroll up to them and led the way to my door at the top of the stairs. As I unlocked it for Lily, Bảo stepped between us, forcing Lily down a step. "He likes to go first in a new place. You mind?"

"No, sure." Appreciating his vigilance, I opened the door and pointed to the hallway light switch. He went in and lit the hall. Then he peeked into the living room, turned in, and found that light. I followed Lily in.

Lily tapped her index finger upon titles along my bookshelves. "You like to read," she said as Bảo flopped on the couch and spread his arms across the back. His eyes lazily wandered the room, but mine snagged on the colorful serape draped behind him. Margo'd been here. I inhaled through my nose for her scent.

"Is that the couch?" Lily asked.

"Uh-huh, yeah," I said, eyes fixed on Margo's serape.

"Who are they?" I heard Lily say.

I looked back, but my eyes skittered off Margo's framed and matted *Girl with Lilies* print above the fireplace before landing on Lily glancing between me and my mantel's photo. "Me, DJ, and Cisco." My *Cisco* slip ignited my face.

She grinned with her lips closed and then extended her hand. "*Tuyết Huệ Thị Nguyễn.* Your name?"

I'd buckled for penalty, but she'd parted her curtain, too. I took her hand as if we'd just met. "L—Les Soze. Ni—Nice to meet you."

She tilted her gaze. "Nice to meet you, 'Les Soze.'"

I'd never heard my name sound so lyrical. "You're not mad?"

"Are you? I didn't tell you my name."

She'd triggered a language lesson from Mai's favorite nun. "Yes, you did. Lily is English for '*Huệ.*'"

She smiled and picked up my picture. "You're a handsome GI. Which one is Cisco?"

I tapped my pal's image. "He's Cisco."

"You protect yourself behind his name. Me, behind my language. Same-same, GI." She chuckled and gently returned our pic to the mantel. Then reached over and picked up Mr. Sapo.

Unlike Sapo's guilty glare, Lily's light came without judgment's burn. "What made you think we were 'same-same' in the first place?"

She replaced Mr. Sapo on the mantel and slightly shrugged. "I didn't. But you said *thank you* in my language and know about my home, Cần Thơ. Made me curious."

"Is that why you invited me to sit with you?"

"You're polite also."

I half smiled. "I told you I liked *chôm chôm.*" But recalling I'd told her I rifled corpses made me list against the fireplace.

"And like now, your eyes fill with memories you try to forget. Like mine."

Lily's tug on our tether strained my frayed tie to Margo. A greasy ambivalence spilled into my belly. I heard my toilet flush.

Lily and I glanced at my empty sofa, then Bảo appeared and leaned against the doorway. Had he heard my Cisco gaff? Out of their flurry of Vietnamese, I caught Bảo's snarling, "Les?"

Lily put her hand up to interrupt him and turned to me. "Time for dinner. Come."

Bảo's scowl sucked the tickle out of her invitation. "My stomach's not right. I'd better stay home."

"You must eat. I bring you something."

I rubbed my belly. "I've got soup, but thanks for offering."

"I hope you feel better. Can I call you when we come for the couch?"

"Sure."

Lily lowered her voice to embellish the obvious. "I need your phone number."

"Oh, yeah." I patted my pockets for a pen. "I'll go write it down for you." I slipped past glowering Bảo to trudge into my bedroom. Ignoring another Margo print hung at the head of my bed, I took my business card and a pen from the nightstand. About to write my home number on the card, I raised my head to funnel in a breath. My eyes locked onto my tux, hung on the outside of my closet door in its transparent bag. The suit's glare pricked my mired fidelity to Margo. I closed my fist. Crushed the card. But I'd promised Lily my sofa—had to give her my number. My fingers fell open. The crumpled card hit the floor. I ripped a piece of paper off a scratch pad and scribbled my home number.

Peering back at my tux, I wanted to believe that once Lily was behind me, I'd prove Margo right and not make her miserable.

Squeezing past Bảo in the dooorway, I handed Lily my number.

She folded it, tucked it into her purse, then dug out one of her business cards. "Where is your pen? I give you my home number."

I shook my head, straining against the tether between us. "I'll call you at work."

Her eyes lingered while she returned her card to her purse. I should've declared my commitment to Margo, but Lily spoke up, "Where is my picture?"

"Oh, ah," I almost said, *hid it*, but managed, "Put it in a safe place. I'll get it."

"Next time." Lily tapped the mantel at the photo of me and the fellas. "Maybe you can put me with you and friends. If you have room."

Lily stepped toward Bảo. "I call when odder brudders can help get couch."

Clumping behind, I asked, "Ah, why the broken English now?"

"I do not have CPA to hide behind in public," she said and chuckled.

I guffawed. Then, took advantage of levity's break to postpone my confession about Margo. It could wait until Lily returned for the couch. It'd be no surprise to her that Margo was more than a best friend. Bảo wouldn't've missed my tux on his way to the bathroom. He'd likely told her already. Not much of a stretch to tie it to the pic I'd sent her.

After Bảo opened the door and stepped through, I asked Lily, "When do you think you'll come for the sofa?" I'd need lead time to steer Margo away. Then I cringed. I hadn't asked for Margo's pic.

She stepped close and gently patted my chest, wafting her lavender scent. "Do not know yet, but I bring you friend picture. Maybe then you say her name."

My voice jumped, "Margo, Margo's her name."

Lily stepped out the door, taking her ghost of a grin with her.

I closed the door behind her, turned and leaned against it. "Phew," purged her scent, but I'd underestimated my attraction to her. I swallowed a breath and grabbed my lighter.

Trudging into my kitchen, I put away Mr. Zippo and reached into the cupboard for the menudo. After my electric opener sliced open the lid, I scooped the gelatinous stew into a generous bowl and zapped it in the microwave. Thankful for the timer's terminal beep, I pulled it out and slurped down the spicy blend, singeing my tongue.

After washing the bowl and spoon, I propped myself up on my arms over the sink and watched the dishwater swirl tripe into the disposal's angry gnash. As spent as my detergent, I wished for a dreamless sleep.

I slogged into my bedroom, slipped off my shoes and socks, and hung up my clothes. Stepping on my crumpled business card, I plopped down on the bed, pulled it from under my toes, and tossed it into my puny wastebasket.

Margo's other framed and matted Diego Rivera print drew my gaze. Taunted by *Man at the Crossroads,* I killed the light and squirmed under the covers.

Fourteen

I rolled over, fumbling the receiver to my ear. "Hello?"

"I'll call back. Didn't mean to wake you."

"Margo. It's fine. I'm awake." I sat up.

"Sure?"

"Yeah, good morning," I said, scooting to the edge of the bed and planting my feet on the floor.

"Mornin'. Sorry to call so early. But I had to know if ya' liked my touches to your casa?"

Glancing up at Diego's print, I pinched my jaw. "*Man at the Crossroads?* Guess I am, huh."

"Look at you, catchin' my psychobabble." She sucked in a hiss. "You don't like it."

"No. I do. Really."

"Would you tell me if you didn't?" After an anxious giggle, she added, "Thought you didn't call me last night 'cause you don't. Almost swung by again when I didn't hear from ya'."

That she'd blamed herself grated my conscience. "I'd tell you."

"Promise?"

"I do."

"Okeydoke. What time ya' get home?"

"Late—late last night." I swore I heard breath escape her nose.

"You should've called me. It's customary for couples to check in with each other, you know."

"Didn't want to bother your Friday night," I droned as guilt sapped the joy out of her love lesson.

"You've got to get over thinking you're a 'bother.' After I left your place, I spent my 'Friday night' charting at the Mission Clinic where I run my group."

She'd been close. "Ah, I don't have that number."

"This is the eighties, *mijo*. I can remotely check my answering machine. Got a pen?"

I grabbed paper and pencil from my nightstand. "Yeah."

"Take my pager and clinic numbers."

I jotted them down.

"Well?"

"'Well?'"

"Ya' ready to part with your bleak couch?"

I forced a match to her bubbly tone. "You mean the one soaking up all the light?"

"That's the one."

"Yeah. Okay. Of course."

"Do I hear second thoughts?"

Her melodic sway pitched my gaze upon my tux. I thanked dumb luck for keeping her away last night and imagined us decked out, strolling hand in hand into the Black and White Ball. Each step further away from Lily and Nam. "No. I'm looking forward to it."

"Then how about I meet you at the Price Club at eleven? I'll get you on my membership, and we can see if they have a sofa you like. You should also get an answering machine."

"Had one. Didn't survive the move."

"Need directions?"

"I have a street map and the yellow pages." Wrung by my guilty fibs, I tempered with a glib, "Two cars again, huh?"

I heard her randy chuckle before she spoke. "Think of it as an incentive." Then she cooed, "If you give up thinking you bother me, we'll share more than a ride the night of the ball."

"A carrot for a jackass," I spouted.

"Les! What'd I just say? I'm not gettin' in the same car with a donkey of doubt."

"Okay, okay. I'll dump my 'donkey' along with the couch."

"Now you're talkin'. See you at eleven."

"I'll be there."

My cheeks deflated with a hiss as I pulled into the parking structure, relieved that Lily'd done her shopping yesterday. My confidence that I wouldn't run into her billowed into excitement at seeing Margo. I parked and waded into the pedestrian stream toward the entrance.

I spotted Margo. Intercepting her at the shopping carts, her sweet peck on my lips sent me into our future together. "Can't wait to drop the two-car rule."

"Me too," she said, turning me around by my elbow and sliding her arm down the inside of mine. She laced our fingers together. "Parking is impossible the night of the ball, and cabs are super busy. I can reserve one to get us there. We'll leave from my place."

She tilted her head into my shoulder. "We'll get back late. Guess you'll have to spend the night."

Imagining it lit a fuse as we took our place in line at Customer Service, but a goose in the butt doused my giddy burn. I turned to the red-faced guy who yanked back his offending weed whacker and struck the woman behind him. He whipped his whacker straight up as he spewed apologies, jerking his head between me and the lady.

She and I traded glances. Both of us denying harm. The poor guy hugged the whacker to his chest.

Margo's giggling danced into my ears to rekindle the Black and White's promise. I followed it into the glow of her sparkling smile.

After securing my membership, we traipsed to their furniture display. I pointed at the little couch I'd looked at last night. "That one looks like it'll fit across from the window seat. What do you think?"

"Like the warm beige." She ran her fingers across its arm. "Nice feel. Guess it's sold, huh?"

Almost, but it'd barely fit until Lily picked up my old one. Stalling, I fingered my chin. "How about we shop around a little?"

Margo's face pinched. "*You* wanna shop?"

I threw up my hands to scatter suspicion. "Didn't complain when you tried on gowns?"

Her glare thawed into a salacious grin. "Only because you thought you'd get a peek at me in my *chones*."

I flopped on the short couch. "Ah."

She tilted her gaze. "Could it be that the longer you wait, the longer you get to keep your old sofa?"

"You're probably right," I said, guiltily pandering to her benign view of my deceit.

"You don't have to give it up if you don't want to."

"No. It needs to go." I snorted a nervous laugh. "But maybe if we shop around a little first, it'll be easier on me."

"Alright, *mijo*. Since we're here, you wanna pick up an answering machine?"

I stood up. "Good idea. How about one like yours with remote access?"

After my successful purchase and enjoying our casual banter, I treated Margo to a Price Club gourmet hot dog lunch.

By the time the club's door monitor checked my receipt to grant us exit, I'd assuaged my conscience by reminding myself that soon Lily'd take my sectional, leave Margo's photo, and be gone along with my ledger of lies.

In the parking garage, Margo dug her keys out of her purse. "I'll take us shopping."

"Dropping the two-car rule?"

"Let's say it's my way of hand-holding while you grieve your sofa."

Despite facing custody in retail purgatory, I said, "I like it. Let's drop my car off at your place."

Margo patted my arm. "Down, Fido. Your car can stay here." Then she stretched up and whispered in my ear, "*Our night* is less than a week away."

I flopped out my tongue in a vibrating pant. She jerked away and whacked my shoulder. "Ay, *perro!*"

After I scooted into her passenger seat, Margo turned to me and said, "Let's go see if our UCLA pic is ready. I'm dyin' to see your expensive frame."

"Tsk. They called. Said they misplaced it."

"No way."

Without a tail to tuck, I ducked my head. "They assured me they'd find it. Promised a discount."

She rocked her head. "They better!"

We spent the afternoon perusing Union Square department stores and boutique furniture shops, so I was more than ready when Margo suggested dinner at her go-to sushi bar. Strolling along, she focused on me from the corners of her eyes. "I can't believe your patience combing through those fabric swatches today."

"You make it tolerable," I said in what felt like an increasingly rare honest reply.

Margo snuggled her shoulder into mine and threaded our arms together. "After sushi, you wanna go get that Price Club couch?"

"Let me wallow in my ambivalence a little longer, okay?" I said, though weary of my deceit.

"Sure, *mijo*. How about after dinner we go back to your place..." she squinted playfully, "in separate cars." Then she grinned and went on, "And I'll help ya' set up your answering machine. It'll be easy since it's exactly like mine."

My mind balked. What if Lily called? I couldn't answer my phone with Margo there. But she'd want to know why I didn't. I wanted to claw out my Zippo, but Margo knew my nervous tell.... Hell, I'd have to get to my bedroom and yank the phone to keep it from ringing. "Deal," I said with all the enthusiasm I could muster against my dread that Lily'd call between opening my door and unplugging the phone.

After dinner, we recovered my car for our solo drives to my place. Arriving at the same time, I insisted she take the space nearest my door. But as I hoofed it to my apartment, I recalled she had a key. I glanced the heel of my hand off my forehead. Would she go in? Answer my phone if it rings?

I saw her waiting at the top of my stairs and put my lighter away. Strolling up, I tucked my answering machine under my arm and brought out my keys. "You didn't use your key."

"Wanted to wait for ya'." Then she drew back her lips. "But, I do gotta pee."

I slipped my key into the lock and opened the door. Margo slipped through.

Raising the answering machine's box, I said, "Meet you in the bedroom."

She turned and rocked her finger. "Okay, but don't get any ideas."

I pinched my face in disappointment but sped into my bedroom. After unplugging the phone from the wall, I slid the nightstand back in front of the empty phone plug and unpacked the answering machine.

Margo found me on the edge of the bed, studying the directions. She sat next to me and reached for the guide. "I know how to do it."

I'd strategically sat between Margo and the wall, so she had me plug in the power cord.

After inserting the message tape, she put her finger on the record button. "Know what you wanna say?"

"Yeah, hit it."

She pressed the red button, and I pinched my nose for its obnoxious effect to distract me from my battered conscience. "You have reached a number that is no longer in service. If you would like to make a call, please hang up and—"

"*¡Ay tu!* Be serious." Margo crossed her arms.

I let go of my nose and raised my hands. "Okay, okay, I'll do it right."

She pressed record again, and I left a bland message. Then she pointed to the steady glow of the machine's LED. "It's ready. It'll blink when there's messages. When I get home, I'll call. Let me leave a message, then call me back to let me know that it worked."

I gave her a thumbs-up, then watched her press her hands into my mattress and wiggle her butt. "Comfy," she said, casting a suggestive smile. Then she shot up, fanning her open fingers. "Better go to the living room." She extended her hand.

I drooped my face. "Do we have to?" But I laced my fingers through hers. She towed me into my living room."

Sitting next to each other on my black beast, she patted the cushion. "Wanna shop around again tomorrow?"

"Why not?"

She shook her head but grinned. Then she suggested we explore south of the city. Citing my apartment's closer proximity to the lower peninsula, she said she'd pick me up and drive again.

I rubbed my palms together. "Oh boy, alone in the same car."

She patted my thigh. "*Cálmate perro*, or we'll take the bus."

"I feel like a kid who can't wait for Christmas," I said, though our delay in sleeping together till Lily's exit eased my conscience.

"You're not the only one, *mijo*."

Her voice danced into my ears, then I watched her gaze land upon my fireplace mantel. "What'd you do with Lily's picture?"

I stammered despite her harmless tone. "I—I took it down until I can gather my Nam pics. Stick 'em in a new album."

Margo leaned back, broadening the scope of her gaze. "Her memory packs a wallop, *mijo*. We should talk about her."

I coughed into my fist. "I'm not over our last 'talk.'"

Margo slid her probing eyes away as if pondering possibilities—suspicions? She fluttered her lashes and tapped her fingertips upon my thigh. "Alright, we'll wait till you're ready."

After meandering around the apartment, discussing more of her decorating ideas, Margo and I strolled hand in hand to her car. The press of our bodies stoked our simmering good-night kiss. "We are on our way, aren't we?" I said, savoring her embrace.

Margo snuggled her cheek into my chest. I felt the purr of her, "Mhmm."

As I watched her drive away, the residual hum of our passionate embrace withered under my beleaguered conscience. At the top of the stairs, after a last click of my lighter, I strolled through the door. Inside, I stuck my head into the living room and glared at my couch. Told myself in less than a week, I'd be free of Lily. I rubbed my cheeks as if to wipe off my deceitful smear.

In my bedroom, I plugged in the phone and hung up my clothes. I'd time for a shower before Margo got home.

Back in my bedroom and in my jeans, I slipped on my UCLA sweatshirt to wait for Margo's test call. Then I lapsed into Margo's observation that Lily's pic packed a punch....Despite its *wallop*, I recalled my relief when Lily said I could keep it. It'd saved me from explaining its disappearance. Reaching up to the closet's shelf, I brought down her photo's hiding place, *The Devil's Dictionary*—to do what?...Say goodbye.

I cracked the pages to her photograph. Her hand blocked the sun's glare from her innocent gaze's reminder of our kinship. I turned away and closed the book. Stashed it back in the closet. Inhaling deeply, I stretched my jaw from side to side.

Startled by a ring, I thought, *Lily?* Then fisted my halted reach—but the shock had exposed Lily's reach. I let the answering machine pick up.

"Hi, *mijo*. Testing, one, two, three. Call me back if it worked. Bye."

I uncurled my fingers and dialed Margo.

Fifteen

Sunday, before opening my door to Margo, I slipped into my bedroom and unplugged the phone. Then I worried about missing Lily's calls. Would she decide I'd reneged on my offer and give up? Toss Margo's pic?

Before we left for the lower peninsula, I snuck back to plug it in for Lily.

When we returned from an otherwise pleasant day, I sweated the moments before unplugging it again, fearful that's when Lily'd call.

I plugged it back in after Margo left.

Disabling my phone added a prickly routine to stalling on a new couch.

Monday, after work, happy to see Margo in my doorway, I spotted her car over her shoulder. "Hey, how come I never land a space across the street?"

She glanced back. "It's the universe telling you it's a hike into the light until you give up your dark sectional."

"Don't start."

Margo laced her arms around my neck, wafting her pristine bouquet. "C'mere, into the warmth of that light."

I threaded my arms about her waist, and we drew our bodies together. After our lingering kiss, she tilted her head, leaving her body snug against a stout Mr. Happy. "Ready to trade the darkness for the light now?"

I pointed at her car. "I can't make you give up your rock star parking. And mine is too far away. How about we pass on the new sofa for now and take a stroll through my new neighborhood?"

She pulled away and spaghetti slapped my shoulder. "Not ready yet, I see."

"Obvious, huh?"

"Ah-huh." After a disappointed smile, she added, "At least we'll exercise."

"I'll throw in dinner—on me."

"Now you're talkin'."

Bedtime came with no word from Lily. I crawled under the blankets and finally fell asleep, wadded up in my sheets.

Tuesday evening, at Margo's suggestion, we roamed Japantown, where she casually pointed out futon furniture. *Hint, hint,* she'd said but didn't scold me for leaving without a buy.

Back home, I felt the strain of my empty answering machine against the Black and White's deadline to annul Lily.

Wednesday, on the phone with Margo, I dangled drinks at the Sunset Lounge to lure her away from shopping. She said she'd only *collude* with my *ambivalence* if we met there in separate cars.

With the Black and White looming, I called Lily's Spa before I left. But Lily wasn't there, dashing my determination to declare my commitment to Margo. I left a message.

Pounding the sidewalk toward my car, I decided I'd cancel the offer if Lily didn't pick up the couch before the ball. I sucked in a shaky breath and took out my Zippo. What if she retaliates and tears up Margo's pic? I rubbed my neck but couldn't see Lily doing that. Click, click. I got in my car and drove off.

Creeping through traffic toward *our place* where I'd suffer interrupting our evening to remotely check for Lily's call back, I found little consolation in my break from shopping.

I arrived before Margo, found stools at the bar with their ocean view, and ordered for us. She came in moments after the perky bartender arrived with our drinks. We hugged and pecked each other's moist lips.

"Sorry, I'm late. Had to swing by the Price Club for a new printer. Place was packed."

I pointed to her chardonnay. "It just got here. Your timing is perfect." I patted the seat next to me. We settled onto our stools, and I raised my beer as she did her wine. Our smiling gazes met above the click of our glasses.

Margo sipped her drink then braced upon her elbow. She squinted. "*Mijo*, there were a couple in line ahead of me. The woman looked like Lily."

The air shrank around me. I feigned a thoughtful look away to untangle my vocal cords. "No—what are the odds?"

The knit of her brow knotted above her nose. "She caught me staring, but I couldn't look away. She didn't either."

"Maybe whoever she was thought you were flirting. This is San Francisco."

Margo slit her gaze. "It felt like she recognized me."

I leaned toward her, and like a hound against a choke chain, I rooted out another lie. "Margo, you always say hidden feelings can blindside you. I know I'd be jealous if some guy's picture hit you like Lily's did me."

A shallow breath escaped her nose as her body deflated. Then she stroked her shoulders.

"Maybe I have ignored my own feelings."

"Ah, yeah?" I said, limp in her reflective gaze.

She glanced away. "I told you I felt rejected when you rented your apartment without me. But I have denied my jealousy over seeing Lily's picture on your mantel instead of our UCLA photo." After a self-deprecating snort, she added, "Today it jumped out to make me think, *That's Lily staring back at me—that she's seen my picture, too.*"

She circled her finger around the rim of her glass. "Left me convinced that you two had found each other....Now I'm as guilty as you for avoiding feelings."

My heart quaked. I wanted to shout, *All you're guilty of is trusting me!* Tell her that I'd panicked at Cupid's threat to our friendship. That I'd been in town but hid in a brothel instead of seeing her, where I'd met Lily—who I didn't have sex with....But I did with Kim—no, I couldn't admit that. Maybe just say it was a spa. Where I got a massage, but not from Lily. Skip sex with Kim to Lily lending me a book with her photo in it. That I'd mailed it back to cut our tie but mixed up our pics. Sent her our UCLA pic....My confessional flurry froze in panic that Margo'd bolt, and I'd never see her again.

Prodded by my conscience, I cleared my throat to hash out a sliver of truth. "Maybe you wouldn't've felt jealous if I'd confessed that in Lily's innocent image, I see what I lost in Nam."

Her body stilled. "That's why her photo hits you so hard." Margo reached over and lit her hand upon my forearm. Her fingers gently massaged my wrist. "Maybe you see it because it's still there."

"It's gone!" I slapped the bar, losing her hand, curled in retreat. A retreat I resoundingly deserved.

Margo didn't release me from her stare. "I wouldn't be here if I didn't see it, too. What do you say to a walk on the beach where we can air out *our* walloping denials?"

Hemorrhaging the truth so close to Lily's exit was a risk I couldn't take. "And end up in Nam?" I shook my head and scrunched my shoulders. "Too much of a hike," I said, my voice withering.

She offered a knowing squint. "One foot is still there, *mijo*. And ignoring what you 'lost in Nam' invites mistakes like I made at the Price Club." She patted my shoulder and left her warm palm there.

I crumpled my face. "I'm the only mistake you've made."

"Stop that! I'm talking about the denial that turned me into a jealous schoolgirl."

I hung my head but glanced between her and my beer. "Don't bring out the best in you, do I?"

Margo fluttered her fingers under her nose. "That smells like you thinking that you made your mom miserable."

I bobbed my head. "Like I'm doing to you now." I pushed up from the bar and slid off my stool.

"Where you going?"

"Nature calls. Be right back."

Margo glanced at my beer. "You've hardly touched it." Then she rocked her head. "You can run, but you can't hide."

I slowed by the pay phone in the restroom corridor. But I couldn't bring myself to check for a message from Lily. I returned and sat next to Margo.

"Ready for that walk?"

"How about after the ball?" Then I added breezily, "You know, once we're *going steady.*"

After a chin-rippling grin, she said, "I suppose we can wait." And then she copied my airy tone, "If I don't catch you with Lily."

Staring out from my petrified pause, I rushed my vocal cords to clone her intended humor. "She's not allowed this close to us going steady. The ball is the day after tomorrow."

I saw no laughter in Margo's blunt stare. Had she seen her unintended bull's-eye in my stymied pause?

Margo sipped her wine and let her eyes wander. A delay while deliberating whether to grant me the benefit of doubt?

She centered her glass upon its coaster and then leveled her gaze with mine. "Once committed, no more postponing that walk on the beach."

I raised my beer. "Okay,"

I got home and trudged into my bedroom. The steady glow of the message light glared, *No Lily.*

Showered, I went to bed to suffer a bumpy sleep.

Sixteen

I closed my office door the day before the Black and White, resolved to call Lily to confess my commitment to Margo, and tell her to come get the couch *now or never*. I picked up the phone, telling myself Lily won't be surprised—not after she and Margo exchanged leers at the Price Club. I dialed her spa.

"Lily's Spa." Lily's melodic lilt muted my resolve.

"It's me, Les."

"Hello, Les." I heard her doorbell. "Moment, please." Footsteps followed, then the harsh buzz of her lock's release.

A man's voice asked for "La-la." It sounded distant. I assumed Lily'd dangled her cordless phone at her side.

"She glad to see you. Half hour or hour today, dear?" Then she must've raised the phone to her ear. "If you alone, I call back. Must take care of customer."

Of course, she'd check if I was with Margo. But it wasn't her professional courtesy that buoyed my mood. It floated upon La-la, *not her* doing that customer. I chided myself for wasting jealousy on a doomed attraction. I told Lily, 'I'm at work.' Gave her my office number.

A few minutes after we hung up, our office manager buzzed me. I broke for the phone. "Les here."

"A Ms. New-yen? On line one for you."

I tapped the flickering button. "Thanks for calling back."

"I call back yesterday. Odder brudder have truck."

I cupped my mouth, then dropped my hand. "Why didn't you leave a message?"

"I see Margo at Price Club. Tenk she go see you."

"Oh—what about tonight?"

"Brudder busy. We come tomorrow."

I stretched the phone away from my billowed hiss. I'd taken tomorrow off to coast into me and Margo's crowning evening. I shook my head. "Come as early as possible."

"We there before you take Margo to Black and White Ball."

Of course, she'd figured it out, but I still stammered like a busted six-year-old. "I—I should've told you."

"Cannot always know what should do," she said, followed by a disarming chuckle. My omission hadn't injured her like it would've Margo. And she'd cast doubt on my commitment to Margo with her, *Cannot always know what should do*. I flagged in my seat.

"I come tomorrow at one?"

All I could muster was, "Okay."

"I bring picture of you and Margo."

Her reminder of Margo's photo pried the phone away from my ear. I pressed it back. "Tha—thanks."

After we hung up, I plodded around my desk to tongue up another guilty score before sitting down to dial Margo.

When Margo answered, I led with, "Guess what?"

"'What?'"

"I donated my couch to a charity. They'll pick it up tomorrow."

"Yay, ambivalence conquered!"

Glad she couldn't see me cringe, I went on, "Yeah. How about Saturday we hit the Price Club for that one?"

"Hmm? Before or after our walk on the beach?" she said, tenderly holding me accountable.

"Your call. I owe you that."

Margo poured on a dulcet resonance, "I guess both depend on us getting out of bed in time."

Her titillating sparkle ignited images of our first night together. "I don't deserve what I'm imagining."

She chuckled. "*Doubt* is on our beach-walk agenda. How about I come over after work to preview you in your tux?"

"Can't wait."

"Hope you didn't forget tennies."

"I did."

"We'll go getcha a pair. See ya'."

I hung up, but my giddy tingle ebbed against the taint of having to unplug my phone while she's here.

Seventeen

I rubbed the sleep from my eyes the morning of the ball. Sitting up on the edge of my bed in my T-shirt and boxers, I gazed at my hanging tux. My new tennies sat upon the floor below, toes out. Just where Margo put them. A sentimental smile subdued my face.

Interrupting my stroll to the bathroom, I detoured down the hall and peered into my living room. Squashed under my ponderous sofa were my hopes that Lily'd be in my rearview mirror by today. But she'd come this afternoon. I straightened up, tugged at the hem of my shirt, and spouted, "In the nick of time." And she'd bring Margo's UCLA pic. I'd get it framed and then poised on the mantel next to me and the fellas, along with Mr. Sapo. Puffing up my chest, I strode into my cramped bathroom.

After my shave, I'd splashed water on a lot more than my face. I wiped up the errant spray and decided it was about time to dust, sweep, and vacuum my apartment.

Back in my bedroom, I slipped on my jeans, made my bed, and tucked my tux into the closet. I slid my tennies in, too, then closed the door.

Dispatching dust and dirt worked up an appetite, but after stashing the vacuum cleaner on the back porch, I toured the place, pleased that I'd made it fit for company.

I donned a clean shirt, put on the new polar fleece jacket Margo bought me, *to fit into the Bay Area,* and headed to my favorite Noe cafe.

My contented tummy and I came home, but as I turned the front door's lock, so twisted my nagging conscience. What if Lily called to postpone the pickup? I rushed into my bedroom.

Relieved by the answering machine's steady LED, my mind eased back to Lily's first visit. I'd offered to show her her picture, but she'd said   *Next time*. That'd be today. I hung up Margo's jacket and pulled *The Devil's Dictionary* from my closet. Opening it to Lily's modest photograph, I wistfully decided that, for her last visit, I'd make room for her on the mantel with my friends. I padded into the living room, holding her photo by its edges, careful not to smudge her.

I stuffed a glaring Mr. Sapo in my pocket before propping Lily's photo against me and my pals' pewter frame. Against Lily's kindred draw, I stepped back and turned to go flop upon my terminal sofa.

Sitting with my back against Margo's serape, my eyes darted between the face of Lily's doomed innocence and my scowl before the same fate. The air grew heavy, hot, and damp. Our images had bored a selfish hole through time to humidify the present. The pungent smell of spent ammo mixed with sizzling vegetation seeped in to mock Margo's warning that the past informed the present—it'd seized it.

A rumble and then a squeal outside from a heavy vehicle's brakes penetrated Nam's grip. I glanced out the window at a large double-parked van and then at my watch. One o'clock, damn!

Expecting Lily, I darted into my bedroom to change into a pressed pair of pleated khakis and a clean polo. The doorbell rang as I tucked in my shirt. "Coming," I yelled before unplugging the phone.

Opening the door to Lily and Bảo, I said, "Hi." Of course, she wore a black business suit, and Bảo's hands were socked deep into the pockets of familiar, olive drab overalls. Too frayed and faded to have come out of Army surplus, I assumed we'd issued them to him before Saigon fell.

"Hello, Les." Her singsong timbre danced into my head, a melody I'd miss. Bảo's grunt? Not so much.

On the street, the van's emergency lights flashed as two more men in crisp overalls hopped out. I stepped aside, allowing Lily and Bảo to pass as the other two men climbed the stairs. Lily introduced us. "Les, this is my brother, *Duy,* and my brother, *Kiên.*"

Duy appeared to be in his early twenties, and Kiên wasn't much older. Neither possessed Bảo's alert eyes. Too young to have been soldiers, they hadn't learned to be wary. Their warm handshakes furthered my presumption.

Bảo impatiently chopped his hand toward the living room doorway, then herded in his sibs.

Lily and I stepped into the room, warmed by unobstructed sunlight. "You need curtains." Then her eyes caught her photo, drawing her toward the mantel.

"Eventually," I said as I went to the couch to rescue Margo's serape before they stripped off the cushions. I carefully folded it, placed it upon the window seat behind, and started helping Bảo remove cushions.

"Let them do it, Les." Bảo and I looked over our shoulders at Lily. After he traded glances with her, he waved me off. I showed him where to disconnect the beast's sections, then joined Lily at the fireplace. She held her photograph in a distant gaze.

"You haven't changed a bit," I said over her brothers' chorus of grunts.

Her eyes glided up to meet mine, accompanied by a forgiving grin that said, *Thanks for the sweet lie.* She laid her pic on the mantel and picked up mine. "Did they take your picture before or after your heart was broken like mine?"

The distant wail of my little girl rose above Lily's brothers' guttural strains.

"Ah….Before."

Lily replaced my photo and leaned hers back against it. Then she stepped close, stirring her lavender bouquet as she brought her eyes to bear upon mine. "I think our broken hearts bring both of us to Lily's Spa."

My commitment to Margo slumped against Lily's kinship. My shoulders drooped.

Lily tenderly patted my chest. A sympathetic touch that forgave my stricken silence. As she stepped back to dig through her purse, I recalled when I'd walked Margo down Mai's deadly path. Her voice had trembled as grief broke her tender caresses. What tortured me wounded her. I doubted it would, Lily.

Lily produced a pen and a business card. "Come to dinner. My house tomorrow." She wrote her address and home number on the back of her card. "Five o'clock."

With my tongue tied against telling her I'd never see her again, I took her card but didn't look at it.

Lily reached back into her purse and then handed me Margo's pic.

My conscience quaked for not asking first. I slid her card and Margo's pic onto the mantel.

She glanced at Margo's photo. "If you can't, I understand."

I crossed my arms and swallowed a breath, but her neutral tone helped me recover a feeble voice. "Thanks."

She tapped the mantel with her finger. "Where is your frog?"

"MIA?" I blurted. But my face simmered, betraying doubt she'd buy that empty answer.

A trace of a smile trimmed her delicate features as her eyes danced thoughtfully as if attending to what she was about to say. But Bảo called out from the doorway, and I realized my sectional had disappeared. He jerked his chin over his shoulder—obviously ready to go.

"I let you go." Lily's tender tone was free of judgment, like her gentle pats.

I followed them to the door, but she stopped and faced me. "Thank you, Les," she said as Bảo offered a single, agreeable nod. He must've liked the couch.

"No. Thank you." I looked away to focus on her exit's release to embrace Margo. "You've done me a favor."

Lily closed the space between us and tiptoed up, wafting her fragrance. Tenderly grasping my shoulders for balance, she delicately skimmed the tip of her daintily inhaling nose across the nap of my cheek. Her uniquely Vietnamese kiss bestowed without a hint of skin contact.

She retreated to her heels, leaving me tingling in her wake. "You are a kind man, Les."

Her praise stole comfortably into who I wished to be, but how could she say that knowing I'd lied to her about Margo? "I wish," slipped out.

She tilted her head while softly patting my chest. "I hope I see you tomorrow."

Båo swung open the door, and she turned away.

I noticed their van had gone. Better to comment on that than her misplaced praise. "Your truck left. How are you getting home?"

"Båo drive me in my car," she said over her shoulder as she followed him down the stairs.

"Oh." I watched them turn down the sidewalk, feeling an odd consolation in Båo's sentinel care of his sister.

I shut the door behind me and went back into my living room. But instead of rushing to replace Lily's pic with Margo's, I sat on Margo's folded serape on the window seat across from the fireplace for a last look at Lily's wholesome image—Sapo? I jumped up, patting my pockets. Oh, yeah. In my jeans.

At the mantel, I grabbed and crumpled Lily's card into my fist and removed her pic—time to seize the moment and get Margo's photo into the hands of a framer.

I dashed into my bedroom, dropped Lily's card on the nightstand, and stashed her photo. I cracked open the yellow pages and jotted down the address of a frame shop, then dug Mr. Sapo out of my jeans.

Back in the living room, I sat Mr. Sapo on the mantel and picked up Margo's photo. There we stood at the entrance to UCLA's sculpture garden. I strolled toward my front door without breaking my gaze, warmed by decades of affection—almost forgot to plug in my phone. I doubled back into my bedroom. Hoped Margo hadn't called.

The framer in his Castro Street storefront politely offered to sell me an off-the-shelf frame for what he referred to as my *snapshot*. But I inspired the artist in him when I asked for his help to properly mount what I expected to become our *heirloom*. His enthusiasm inflated along with the expense of his custom-bordered, double-matted, beveled aesthetic. And he promised to complete his creation by Wednesday.

I drove home, relieved that if Margo asked, I could tell her that *our* UCLA pic had been found. That it'd be ready the middle of next week. But walking from the car, I caught a drift of Lily's bouquet. My heart stumbled. I needed to strip, bathe, and wash these clothes. And what if Margo had tried calling without the answering machine kicking on when Lily was there? Then called back after I'd plugged it in and could leave a message. I'd have to explain all that. I reached for my lighter. Click, click.

I stomped up my stairs to the din of my Zippo. In my bedroom, I stripped and stuffed my khakis and polo into a dry-cleaning bag. Hazarding a glance at my answering machine, its steady glow teased that Margo hadn't called. At least not since I'd plugged it in.

I plodded off to the shower. But with Lily behind me, just a few more sanitizing fibs were left to erase her threat.

Washed and wrapped in a towel, I returned to my room and into the jabs of my message light. It had to be Margo. Feeling exposed, I changed into my jeans and T-shirt before I pressed play.

"Hi, *mijo*. Just checkin' in. Call me." That her bubbly enthusiasm wasn't that of a Grand Inquisitor welcomed my finger to target her number.

"Hello."

"It's me," I said, then coughed into my fist.

"Nervous cough, *mijo*?"

Damn, how long before guilt let go? "Ah, busted. This is a big night."

"It's our 'big night.' And you're not the only anxious one." After a tight giggle, she went on, "I called earlier. You didn't answer, and when your answering machine didn't pick up, I thought, *Oh my God, he's run off with Lily.*"

Ducking behind her nervous titter, I spouted, "Who?" Then followed with a nasally chortle.

"Good answer!"

I quickly added, "I'd tripped over the phone cord. Didn't realize it'd disconnected till a while ago. You must've just called back while I showered."

"See?" Then her voice bumped between chuckles. "My jealous stumble goes to show you you're not the only one trippin'."

"Ha!"

Her voice dipped into a tentative drone. "Did you donate your couch today?"

"Gone. Finally." My inflated glee masked the bite of Lily's reduction to donee.

"Yay! How 'bout you come early for a celebratory toast? I'll make us a bite to eat, and you can change into your tux here."

Her voice cantered into a salacious purr. "I might even let you help me slip into my gown. You know, get you *In The Mood*, the ball's theme."

"Ruff-ruff!"

"*Ay perro!*"

"On my way." I hung up as desire jumped the fire lines of my loins, flaring my heart. I packed an overnight bag, slipped into my new tennies, put on my polar fleece over a pressed long sleeve, and grabbed my tux.

Springing along toward my car with the tux draped over my shoulder, I imagined the formal waving behind like a victory flag.

Eighteen

Apparently, no SF neighborhood could boast of convenient parking. I'd hiked blocks to Margo's second-story condo. Panting, I rang her bell.

She opened up greeting me with her broad smile. "Come in, *mijo*."

I stepped into her home where "*Oye Como Va*" cha-cha'd into my ears. Her blanketing hug and wet smack on the lips vaporized my weariness. "Here, let me go hang that up for you." I handed her my tux. Then she reached for my overnight bag. "I'll put that in my bedroom, too."

I closed the door behind me as she turned and pranced down her hall with my gaze in tow.

"There's a cheese platter on the coffee table. Go dig in," she said over her shoulder.

But I couldn't turn away from her halter top that ended above the mouth of her deliciously snug jeans, exposing the naked contours of her caramel waist. I followed her modest sway until it rocked loose visions of Lily's supple hips. I lurched into the living room, where I snagged my toe on her Persian rug. "Oof!"

"You okay?" I heard from down the hall.

"Tripped on your rug,"   I said, catching my balance. "Didn't fall!" I stiffened up and focused on her grape-garnished dairy delights.

"Careful."

Gingerly stepping across the rug, I slipped off my jacket and draped it over one of her armchairs. Gazing at Margo's own serape-draped sofa across from the chairs, I dismissed Lily's intrusion. Even with Lily behind me, it'd take time for her aggrieved heart to stop haunting mine.

I eased down on the couch and popped a green grape in my mouth. Then with a multi-grain cracker in one hand, I waved an *hors d'oeuvres* fork over an array of bit-sized candidates.

"*Mijo*, come open the champagne." Her holler interrupted my stab at a Gouda. "We gotta toast to your dearly departed couch."

"Let's do that. Coming."

I slowed through her dining room to admire her wall's feathered pre-Columbian masks. Iridescent peacock plumes waved welcome as I passed.

Margo handed me a chilled bottle of Perreir-Jouët in the kitchen, a drink as serious as our anticipated night. "Whoa. Classy."

"It's a 'classy' night. Pop that over the sink while I get my crystal flutes and ice the chiller."

I twisted off the *muselet*, then popped the cork. The damned cork ricocheted off the ceiling striking her frig door where she scooped ice. I grimaced. "Sorry."

"Ya' missed."   Between giggles, she added, "Gimme the bottle and grab those flutes off the island."

We strolled into the living room, where Margo parked her copper ice bucket and stood next to her couch, then stopped me from sitting.

"The sacrifice of your bleak sectional deserves a standing salute." She lifted the artsy bottle. "Here, let me pour the honors." She filled my offered flutes and returned the champagne to the ice.

I handed her her bubbly.

Facing each other, we raised our flutes, but Margo hesitated from clicking hers on mine. "What's your farewell toast?"

"In the nick of time!" I tilted my glass toward hers.

Margo sharpened her squint. Held her glass dead-still.

Had she caught the temper of Lily's last-minute exit? I veered into my attachment to the couch and spouted, "Hey, I gave myself till today to dump it."

She fluttered her eyes, then let her grin overtake them. She tapped her glass to mine, and we watched each other sip. Then Margo raised her glass again. "To the first day of *our* new beginning."

I heartily clicked her rim. "To a dream come true."

We eased down on her sofa together and couldn't've choreographed it better. Our eyes met while we softly landed our flutes upon her glass coffee table. I could taste her tantalizing scent as our hands trailed up each other's arms, drawing us close. Our parted lips touched, inviting our tongues into their deliciously wet duet. Fire spun into my greedy loins.

Caressing the contours of Margo's lithe body, my hand skirted the diameters of her breasts until she guided my hand upon one of her erect nipples. Then her fingers slid down to massage Mr. Happy's conspicuous swell.

I began tugging at her blouse. Margo tore at my belt buckle but gasped, "*Mijo*, we won't make the ball if we don't stop."

I released her blouse but felt an odd relief, disappointing a determined Mr. Happy.

Margo's voice fell, "I'd be okay with that." She stroked the inside of my thigh.

As much to explain to myself as to Margo my odd chill, I said, "Thought we were saving our first night together as the *crowning event* to tonight's ball?"

Margo cooed, "I didn't know you were such a romantic— love it!" She fanned her face with both hands. "Whew," she added and then turned to dollop fig jam upon a slice of Cheddar. She offered it to me on a cracker. I grinned, then opened wide. She slid her savory treat upon my tongue.

"Come on, let's have dinner. Know you like cheese enchiladas," she said and patted my knee.

"Oh boy!" I rubbed my stomach, and we traipsed into the kitchen.

"Did I tell ya' that the ball raises money for SF Symphony's education program?"

She hadn't, but after she'd adjusted her oven's temp, her excited explanation and anticipatory review of the evening's events confirmed my wisdom in not missing the soiree. After I offered to help her set the table, she handed me plates and napkins and followed me with knives and forks.

"The first thing we do when we get there is get our dance cards."

"'Dance cards?'" I adjusted the last napkin by its plate.

"Yeah, more than a program. Tells us when and where the artists are performing *and* what kinds of *comida* we'll find there. I do know that Dinah Shore's only set is at nine. Don't wanna miss dancin' to Dinah."

"I guess if you call what I do dancing?"

Giggling, Margo sputtered, "And who better to dance to, to *shore* up your confidence?"

Chuckling, I said, "Clever, cute."

"She's playing at Davies Symphony Hall. The Henry Moore sculpture is right in front. The perfect place to meet if we lose each other."

"'Lose each other?'"

She turned toward the stove and spoke over her shoulder. "It's easier than you think. People get lost in the thick crowds all the time."

She placed a hot casserole on a braided mat on the table. "Grab the salsa outta the frig while I get the rice and beans."

We sat across from each other, and Margo squinted a playfully suspicious leer. "On top of getting lost, what if I did see your Lily at the Price Club? Tonight, I wander off to the lady's room, and lo and behold, she springs out of your past, and you two get swept away by—" Margo tapped her temple with her index finger, "your reunion."

I slouched in my seat, then popped straight up, tossing my hands. "Margo!"

Giggling, she reached across the table. "Can't help being jealous. She's so pretty."

Lacing my fingers through hers, I dismissively shook my head.

Margo squeezed my hand then let go. "Time's flyin'. Let's eat." She scooped an enchilada out of the casserole onto my plate.

After dinner, I washed the dishes, and Margo dried. Toweling the last dish, Margo nudged my shoulder with hers. "We should get dressed, Leslie Soze." She followed her titillating tempo with a suggestive grin. "Would you like to join me in my bedroom to change?"

"Whoa? Is this a test of my resolve?"

"Consider it a preview of what's to come." She reached for my hand. "Come on."

Eagerly taking her hand, she towed me along, rocking her head as she wispily sang, "Getting to know you, getting to know me."

She led me into her bedroom. I noted an array of candles on her furniture, all as colorful as her southwestern bedspread. Some in glass, others free-standing pillars, still others as delicate pucks blossoming at the tips of wrought iron stems. As she carefully laid our formals upon her bed, I imagined our naked bodies exploring each other, bathed in candlelight.

"Ready?"

"For?" I said, shaking off my thermal muse.

"Follow my lead." Margo pulled her halter top up and off, exposing the lacy support of her dainty breasts. Then she unbuttoned her pants, but while peeling them down, she caught my leer. "*Ay, perro*, don't stare. Strip to your *chones,* then put your suit on."

"Had to make sure your '*chones*' matched your fuchsia bra."

She slapped the air between us, and I shifted my attention to Lakers' basketball. Had to tame a rigidly attentive Mr. Happy to slip my jeans past him. "By the way. DJ wants a picture of the princess and penguin."

"Already loaded my camera." She slipped into her gown and turned her back to me. "Zip me up?"

Snug in my tux, in all but its jacket and aglow in the heat of our intimacy, I carefully zippered what she'd defined as her *blush-hued* gown.

Margo took a step away, twirled around, and swooped back to peck my lips. Then she patted my chest, conjuring Lily's tender touch. I tensed.

"What was that?"

"Surprise?"

"Sounds like a question."

I looked down and adjusted my cummerbund. "Must be jitters at stepping past the security of our friendship."

After a reflective pause, she said, "Add that to our beach-walk's list." She turned to her closet and slid her bolero jacket off its hanger. "Here, help me on with this."

I held it as she threaded her arms through. "This going to keep you warm enough tonight?"

She faced me again and smiled. "That's your job. Come on. Let's take DJ's picture before we go."

Nineteen

Margo and I hopped out of the cab, got our Dance Cards, and coursed our way through the crowds to find Moore's art. Bursts of laughter from a passing gaggle made it difficult to hear. "You weren't kidding."

She cocked her ear toward me.

I cupped the corners of my mouth. "You weren't kidding about the crowds." I watched my frosty breath scatter.

She tugged my shoulder down and aligned her lips to my ear. "Look around. Ya' see everything from chic gowns to creative consignment-shop wraps. Don'tcha love it?" Margo rubbed her shoulders and raised her voice. "Let's go warm up to Dinah."

We strolled into Davies Symphony Hall and heard Ms. Shore's rich voice cresting above her big band's flourishing swing. Margo tore me away from my bite on a chicken medallion. "Snack later. Time to put the good foot down."

We melted into the anonymous crowd, where my robotic bounce mixed with other stiffs lurching like clumsy jugglers. Though Margo's hypnotic sway kept me on the floor for the whole set.

As we clapped among hollers of "encore," I leaned down to bellow, "You know, I could see Pop in a zoot suit twirling Mom around to Tommy Dorsey." Then I squinted lasciviously. "But I can't imagine any girl as sexy as you romping to the music."

"*Ay tu.*" Margo threaded her arm around my waist for a side hug. "Can't cool down now. Time for salsa."

We sauntered our way into the Opera House lobby, holding hands. Oreo cookies anchored black and white balloons to tables of tapas, mushroom quesadillas, and flan. Margo stretched ahead as I lagged to reach for a quesadilla. Without letting go of my hand, she turned to come stand next to me. "Didn't I feed you enough?"

I nodded with a mouth full, swallowed, then said, "Couldn't pass it up."

A lively salsa filled the air, but I towed Margo behind in my break for the bar.

"You better ask me to dance before somebody else does."

I waved for the bartender. "First, a little agave grease for my step."

Margo clicked her tongue but playfully glared. "I'll have champagne."

I ordered a tequila shot along with Margo's bubbly.

Behind her, a dapper silverback shouldered his way into the bar as our drinks came. "May I have this dance?"

She glanced at him, then at me, but before she could speak, I said, "Go on, it'll give me time to down a dose of jiffy lube."

"Okay," she said to him over her shoulder, but she poked me in the chest, just as our drinks arrived. "You're off the hook for one song. Then, no more excuses."

Her finger had landed harder than Lily's merciful pats. But I managed to raise my shot glass and nod. "I'll be ready."

She broke her gaze, took the guy's arm, and strolled off. I felt a jealous prick, so slammed back the shot. Then, I scooted it toward the bartender for another dose. I gulped it down and turned, but I'd lost Margo somewhere in salsa's pulsing bipedal stew.

Scanning for Margo, I sipped at another shot as the tune ended. She emerged from the crowd alone, fanning herself as she strolled up to me.

"Where's my competition?"

After her pressed smile, she said, "He got his dance. And I let him know it wasn't a *chance* at anything else."

I followed my relieved chuckle with, "What a reassuring rhyme."

She reached up, took away my shot glass, and tilted her head toward the dance floor. "Break's over."

Her bubbly tone aired nicely upon tequila's frisky sparkle. "I'm ready," I said as the band fired up another tune.

After confidently aping Margo's graceful repertoire until the band's break, I offered my elbow. "Worked up an appetite yet?"

Margo grinned and hooked her arm through mine.

We threaded our way outside to weave through the crowds and sample the street's tented culinary treats. After satisfying our tummies and guided by our dance card, we indulged some blues, a little rock, and even a sample of Sinatra. I repeatedly thanked Margo for reminding me to wear tennies.

After a Zasu Pitts Memorial Orchestra set at the Civic Auditorium, Margo snuggled next to me and, in a honeyed tone, suggested, "If we leave a little early, it'll be easier to get a taxi ride into *our new future*."

Hugging each other against the evening's chill, we ambled to Franklin Street and hailed a cab. I opened the back door, and Margo scooted in. Sliding next to her, I came face to face with Black Tooth drooling at Margo. A feverish blush consumed my face.

His eyes darted between Margo and me before an evil grin darkened his face. "It's you! Guess you're not seein' your other girlfriend tonight."

I sprung back out, grabbing Margo's hand. "Not this guy, Margo." She stretched to the curb behind me. I slammed the door, and he peeled out. Left us gagging on scorched rubber.

Margo stroked and rolled her shoulder. "'Other girlfriend?'"

I bent at my waist, arms akimbo, and stirred truth with fiction. "He took me to see my apartment, but gum from his duct-taped seat ruined my slacks. I didn't tip him." I turned my back, looking over my shoulder. Any gunk on my pants?"

She looked me up and down. "Don't see anything."

"Turn around, how about on your dress?"

She slightly turned but kept her eyes on me.

I walked around her. "You're okay."

She crossed her arms. "He said *other girlfriend*, not cheapskate."

I swooped up my hands. "Tsk. Meaner to ruin it with you than call me cheap."

She tilted her head but fluttered her eyes as if deciding to believe me or not. After a slight pinch of her face, she dropped her arms. Margo spread her fingers and reached. "C'mon, let's grab a cab and get out of the cold."

Holding her hand, I stepped into the gutter where I belonged and hailed another taxi. Margo slid in, and I followed. She gave the driver her address, adjusted her gown, then leaned her head upon my shoulder.

The warmth of her body thawed my guilty frost. "Here, let me do my job and warm you up." I slid my arm around her. She snuggled into my shoulder. As the cab eased away from the curb, I hoped I'd left behind the last of my antiseptic lies.

Chuckling through my nose, I said, "I'll tell ya', those black and white balloons tied down by Oreo Cookies were the highlight of my night. Can't get more creative than that."

Margo clicked her tongue, then stroked my thigh while praising my tequila-lubed dancing, "For enthusiasm if not style."

I jerked back, fingers splayed, "Whaddaya mean?"

We lofted into reliving our evening's giddy highlights. Crescendos of laughter filled our ride home.

Margo opened her door and turned on the light. Looking over her shoulder, she said, "Here we are." Her voice sparkled in sync with her emerald eyes.

I followed her in, and she turned to drape her arms around my shoulders. Mine met around her waist. I kicked her door closed as our kiss melted our bodies together in a feverish embrace. Margo tilted back to bring the back of her hand against an exaggerated yawn. "Time for bed? Ya' think?"

I patted my mouth, quavering my fake yawn. "If only I can make it that far."

Margo took me by the hand. "Here, let me help." She led us down the hall into her bedroom.

She pulled out two candlelighters from a nightstand drawer and handed me one. "I'll light the ones on the nightstands, and you take the vanity ones." She pressed play on her bedside stereo.

The romantic bolero *"Sabor a Mí"* drifted into my ears as I brought flame to wicks. Margo turned the lights off, leaving the mercurial flicker of open flames. I turned to see her next to her bed, her back to me. She draped her hair behind her ear. "Help me with my zipper?" She tilted her head to expose her neck.

I swooped upon her, my wet kisses following the contours of her neck. Inhaling her scent, my fingers parted her zipper. Her gown puddled to the floor. Layers of my tux soon followed.

Our lips found each other, first in careful, tender pecks. Then our greedy tongues danced into each other's mouths as wet, swollen passion laid us upon her bed.

I clumsily peeled off Margo's fuchsia lace as she did my bulky boxers. She pushed my head between her firm breasts. My mouth slid between her delicious nipples, nibbling one and then the other.

"*Que rico*," she purred.

"Oh, Lily," I whispered.

She kicked out from beneath me, scurried under the covers, and sat against the headboard. "That cabbie busted you tonight." Her arms clamped her knees to her chest. "I did see '*Lily*.' Didn't I?"

Prone and flaccid, with Lily's name throbbing in my ears, *"Believe me when I say how much I love you,"* sailed out of the stereo. Margo slapped it off.

Mute and as naked as my duplicity, I slid to the floor on my knees and patted the ground for my underwear. I struggled with weighted limbs to slip back into my shorts and pants. Margo reached across the bed, snapping her fingers in my face. "Answer my question."

As defeated as my lies, I stood slouched and fumbled to button my disheveled shirt. "Ahem. Probably."

Margo poked her finger at her vanity's chair. "Sit over there. And blow out the candles."   She switched on her nightstand's lamp and blew out her candles.

Amid the funk of extinguished flames, I straddled the chair, keeping its back between us.

Margo leaned back against the headboard. "Did you just meet her? Is that why I never saw her picture before?"

Squirming under her strict glare, I whined my cowering defense. "Yeah, but I thought you and me were just friends at that time."

"When—'that time' you came and told me your company was moving?"

I dropped my gaze. "No. After that visit, where you first hinted at romance, I'd come home and had a horrible nightmare about losing you. Then I was sent back here on business. Torn between my love for you and its threat to our friendship, I'd panicked. I snuck into town without telling you."

I looked up and saw her deflate.

"How'd you meet her?" she asked as if only to herself. Then, her eyes wandered into mine.

"By accident."

"Don't be evasive—where?"

"She…she owns a spa."

"You at a 'spa?'"

She deserved the truth, but I couldn't hazard bachelorhood's decadent details. "I was tensed up avoiding you. I—I went for a massage."

"She gave you a massage and her picture?"

"Not the massage. But we talked about Vietnam, and she lent me a book. Her picture was in it."

Margo looked away. "And you displayed her on your mantel." She jerked back and glared. "She's been to your apartment. Saw our picture—she *did* recognize me at the Price Club."

"She didn't see your picture at my apartment." I rubbed my face. "Once I knew you'd given us a chance to be together, I knew her and I couldn't be friends."

"'Friends?'"

"Yeah, I—I mailed back her book. With what I thought was her photo." I hissed in a breath. "But I'd mixed up our pic with hers and sent it to her."

Margo shook her head. "Your Freudian slip ejected my picture."

"I was wrapping her book to mail it when the guy showed up to install my phone. Got distracted, is all."

"You telling me she hasn't been in your apartment?"

My gaze fell to the floor. "Only twice, but just to—"

"'Twice!'" she flared, and I glanced into her blistering glare.

"I felt guilty for starting a dead-end friendship—gave her my sofa."

"What?" she spat.

"She came by once to see it and then came back to pick it up."

Margo raked her fingers through her hair. "It was Lily you couldn't let it go of, not your couch. I can't tell what shatters me more. Me letting you convince me that Lily was a part of your past or how much she means to you now."

"Margo, I met her before I knew you'd dropped your guard."

"Then lied to hide her after you did," she said, her voice seething.

"Only long enough to get our picture back and cut her loose." I quavered in a breath. "There's nothing between us."

"Except her whispered name 'between' my breasts." Margo's voice crumbled.

I watched tears spill down her cheeks and said, "She's gone now."

"'Gone?'" She dabbed her eyes with her blanket. "Or, 'Lily' escaped your lips to stop you from making love to the wrong woman."

I looked away. Barely able to lift my voice beyond a whisper, I said, "That can't be. What can I do to fix us?"

"'Us?'"

Her dismissive chill pierced my bones. Deserving her punishing loss, I said, "I'll go." I stood up, went by her bed, and bent down to pick up my jacket and cummerbund.

I turned toward the rustle of covers. Margo had slid off the bed and went to her closet, where she wrapped herself in a terry cloth robe. She sputtered through her sodden throat, "Uh-uh. You're not off the hook. You're on the couch."

She pulled bedding from a shelf, came over, and shoved a blanket and pillow into my chest. "Go make your bed. See in the morning if you can convince us both that I'm who you belong with."

I stepped into the hallway, and she shut her door.

Numb, I wandered down the hall into a living room anemically lit by an outside streetlight. I plopped down on her sofa with her bedding on my lap. She hadn't thrown me out. Gave me a chance to persuade her that Lily's behind me. But she'd said, *convince us both.* She thinks I'm fooling myself.

Squeezing my eyes shut, I pinched the bridge of my nose only to relive the hostile snaps of Margo's fingers in my face. My eyes fluttered open and darted about the shadowy walls. In the morning, Margo'd sift through my broken lies. Hammer at her charge that I'd almost made love to the wrong woman. What if she's too mad to believe I hadn't?

I set her bedding aside. Tiptoeing into her kitchen, I rummaged through drawers for a pen and notepad. Finding only a pen, I wrote on a paper napkin that I left, afraid that the wounds I'd inflicted were too raw to confront without completely ripping us apart. Begged her to see my *flight* as a cowardly attempt to let her heal enough to tolerate my pleas for forgiveness. That I'd do anything to repair what we had. I signed, but the drag of my name tore the flimsy paper.

I left my torn note upon her bedding, weighted down by my key to her door. I grabbed my polar fleece and kept my Zippo quiet until I hit the sidewalk.

Somehow, I made it home through the shards of my shattered dream. In my bedroom, I tossed my clothes over the back of a chair, letting them fall where they may. I crawled under the covers into the barbs that DJ might never get his picture of the princess and the penguin.

Twenty

The phone rang early, once. But awake, I grabbed it—too late. It'd be just like Margo to call to confront my leaving. Not like her to hang up with second thoughts. A second thought I didn't deserve.

I sat up on the edge of the bed. Assuming she'd called, I dialed her number, though I'd no excuse for leaving except my plea of cowardice. It rang repeatedly, and her answering machine didn't pick up. "Humph," I said and tongued away the ironic taste of my own medicine.

Rubbing my eyes, I lapsed back between Margo's breasts, whispering Lily's name. She'd kicked out from under me. Then accused me of almost making love to the wrong woman. I planted my elbows upon my thighs and propped my cheekbones into the heels of my palms.   Staring at the floor, I recalled Lily and me at the Price Club, where I'd lost control of her allure, and gushed, *Hey, you want my couch?*—I'd made sure to see her again. Then, at my apartment, my tongue slipped to rid Cisco's name out from between us.

Pressing my hands into the mattress, I pushed up, but my elbows gave. My ass fell under the weight of the evidence against me—had I nearly made love to the wrong woman?

Under the glare of Margo's *Man at the Crossroads*, I twisted and gaped at her prophetic print. If I'd stayed at Margo's, my attempts to deny Lily wouldn't've survived her scalpel *mentis*. Her love for me wouldn't have either. My lungs stalled.

In with my next, quavering breath fluttered a battered hope. Had whispering *Lily* stopped miscarried sex from gutting all of Margo's affection as cheated sex did from Dr. Mentiroso? Had I been right to give Margo's wounds time to heal in order to tolerate forgiveness? Then I recalled an ancient Greek's warning, *Hope's hand, hovering over the urn of mercy, left it empty.* Crossing my arms, I shoved my fingers into my armpits and hissed in a long breath.

Feeling the morning chill, I stood up to get my jeans but remembered I'd left them at Margo's. With one hand massaging my caustic gut, I opened the closet and reached for a pair of pants. Then a shirt. I'd no idea of what to do after buttoning my shirt.... Maybe breakfast? But Margo's forgiveness was a hunger food couldn't satisfy. After slipping into a gray sweater, I slinked out of my apartment to escape Margo's decor.

Clumping along under a crisp blue sky to the tempo of my lighter, I didn't expect to escape my gloom. Made me think that leaving the ball without dancing to a tune we'd made our own forecasted the disaster. I snorted out loud.

During my aimless wandering, I ended up in the Mission District, where I forced down a street taco to silence my gut. Tossing my wadded-up trash into a can, I recalled Lily's crumpled card on my nightstand. I hadn't read her address but hadn't trashed it either.

Eventually, rounding a corner near my car, I headed over to grab my street maps.

Back home, sitting on my bed, I picked up Lily's card and parted its creases to her Oakland address. She'd invited me to her home despite nailing my date with Margo. Said she'd understand if I couldn't come. I felt her forgiving pat on my chest.

Twenty-one

Though I hadn't eaten more than that taco by the time I left for Lily's, it wasn't her dinner offer that drew me. Her merciful pats upon my chest had.

I sped along the Bay Bridge, but a sense of doom strummed among the flickering shadows of the lower deck. I'd lied to Margo and myself about my attraction to Lily. Left her as miserable as my mom. What else do I hide from myself that'd pop out to injure Lily, too? I gulped a breath as I entered the tunnel through Yerba Buena Island. I'd spare Lily. Turn around.

Out the tunnel in sight of Oakland, the tentacles of my about-to-be-stranded heart latched on to how Lily hides her real name. Like I hid behind Cisco's. How her invitation came after she'd exposed my date with Margo.... Where my deceit left Margo bleeding, Lily forgave without insult. I missed the first exit. Then the next.

Lily's neighborhood felt familiar. Like Los Angeles, the houses had yards, and convenient street parking was available because families weren't stacked one on top of another. I drove by her generous, ranch-style home. The beige house sat back from the sidewalk, surrounded by a low wooden fence that enclosed a manicured lawn. A couple of oak trees stood on either side of a pavestone path to the door. A wooden park bench sat in the shade of one. I made a U-turn and parked across the street.

A half-dozen squealing kids chased each other around the yard. Hysterical giggles streamed from four little girls, pursued by two half-pint boys. I rechecked the address before opening the gate.

Halfway to the house, a brown-haired girl rushed me, grabbing my pant leg. She sidestepped around me to evade her pursuer.

A goose-stepping, straight-armed Frankenstein rammed my opposite thigh. Sweet memories of Mai jarred loose. But young Frankenstein's impact knocked me off balance. Like a desperate Quasimodo, I hunched over, twisting my arms to keep the youngsters and me from toppling.

Just as I was sure to fall, the girl pushed off, pitching a scream. They left me standing and grinning. The rims of my eyes damp with Mai's playful memory.

I wiped my eyes and turned up the path to see Bảo at the front door. I suspected he'd tracked the drone of my engine when I made my U-turn.

We shook hands, and he guided me into a living room energized by another throng of silky-haired children. We waded through a clutter of toys and books I recognized from the Price Club. Bảo announced something to the kids in a mixture of Vietnamese and English. Out of it, I understood, "Auntie Lily, friend."

"Hi," I said, which resulted in one "Huh," a couple of waves but had no effect on two tangling sumos.

Bảo led me into a hallway past a large dining room with its table set for a banquet. I cupped my pleased guffaw at a kids' mini table with matching place settings.

Fragrances of mint and cilantro tickled my nose as we passed a kitchen the size of my apartment, and I caught a glimpse of Lily and three other women busily preparing dinner.

We entered a den crowded with people, and there sat my sectional. From a small stereo next to a Buddhist altar drifted the polyrhythmic sway of an organ. The Doors' "Light My Fire," of course.

Bảo introduced me to a dizzying array of friends and relatives, and I was welcomed by Duy's and Kiên's hearty handshakes. At the opposite side of the room stood Lily's "masseuse," Kim, chatting with another woman. Her tasteful pantsuit bore no hint of her sensual vocation. But her eyes met mine, and my face burned as if everyone could see I'd paid her for sex. She waved hello as casually as if we'd met at church. Hers and everyone else's smiles helped cool my cheeks, but their sing-song greetings laced among the kitchen's aromas spun my chronometer back to Nam.

Lily strolled in, dish towel in hand, wearing a clean, though faded granny dress. That sixties error in chronology didn't help reset my clock.

"Hello, Les. I'm glad you came."

I could only nod while trying to untangle my tongue, snagged between time zones.

She took me by the hand into the kitchen, where she introduced me to her mother, Mrs. Nguyễn, and to *Anh* and *Cam,* Duy's and Kiên's wives. Their warm welcomes in English helped restore the present along with my voice.

Mrs. Nguyễn took Lily's towel and said she'd take over, adding, "Go talk in den."

Lily led me around the large coffee table in front of the sectional. When a couple rose so that we could sit, I tried to stop them. But they spoke to Lily in Vietnamese. She turned to me, "They are going to check on the children." She sat and patted the seat next to her.

No one had been introduced as Lily's father. Fumbling between ignoring a painful loss or asking, I clumsily said, "Did your father make it here?"

Her eyes didn't meet mine, but I recognized her insular gaze as she lifted her words, "My father was old. Did not want to leave ancestors." She took in a breath before her eyes found mine. "He died in his sleep before the rest of family follow me here."

"I'm sorry," I said, but the little girl who'd used me for an obstacle outside rushed in between the table and sofa.

She flung herself between Lily's legs and wrapped her arms around her waist. Lily chuckled, "Annie, this is Mommy friend, Les."

Annie turned, snuggled her cheek into Lily's tummy, and smiled. Her innocent grin invited more sweet memories of Linh Mai.

"We've met. Haven't we?" I said to Annie and realized that pools of blue shimmered within the contours of her graceful eyes. Except for her eye color and brown hair, Annie was the image of her mother.

Annie nodded, burrowing further between her mother's hips. Lily untangled a snarl from Annie's hair.

I told Lily about our Quasimodo episode outside. The little one turned around and, using her mother's legs for support, raised her feet from the floor as she checked me out. Lily lifted her to her lap and kissed the top of her head.

"Annie start kindergarten this year." Then Lily began telling me how Annie speaks English and Vietnamese. She rippled her brow, "Do you think talking two languages is a problem at school?" But Annie shrieked, "I'm gonna get you," and leaped off her mother's lap.

I jerked to dash after her as if she were Mai, then shrank, embarrassed.

Lily patted my knee. My eyes met her approving grin, and she asked me again, "What do you think?"

"They're a gift. Not a problem."

Lily's chest rose, but before she could speak, her mother came out of the kitchen and announced that dinner was ready in Vietnamese and then English.

We merged with the crowd toward the dining room, frequently hobbled by the corralling of stray kids.

"Mommy!"

I turned to the boy's yelp to see young Frankenstein spin and back into Kim. He thrust up his arms, and Kim braided her fingers into his as he perched his feet upon hers. She goose-stepped toward dinner. Touched by how she'd harbored love for her son despite its abandon from retail sex, I thought her heroic but dropped my gaze to the floor. I'd sacrificed all my love for commercial sex until my debacle with Margo.

Lily sat me down at the adult table but excused herself and turned for the kitchen. Over her shoulder, she asked if I ever ate Vietnamese raw beef.

Recalling the zesty Vietnamese version of carpaccio, I blurted, "*Bò tái chanh!* Love it."

She looked away, shaking her head. "I think you're Vietnamese in another life—chopsticks?"

I glanced down. My place setting was the only one with silverware. "Of course."

"Juice, beer, wine?"

"Juice. *Cảm ơn.*"

She looked back again, smiling. "You're welcome."

Lily left me immersed in the children's innocent laughter and the buzz of parents attempting to shuffle them toward their tiny table. Plunged into what I'd missed as Pop's only child, a sad yearning to belong surfaced, but it bubbled away in the giggles around me. Relaxing against the back of my chair, I didn't know about being Vietnamese in a past life, but I felt comfortable here.

Lily reappeared with her mom and sisters-in-law, carefully weaving around kids to deliver bowls of aromatic herbs and sauces in hues of red and silky brown. Cam carried plates of pink, paper-thin slices of beef smothered beneath slices of lime, chopped mint leaves, and minced peanuts; *bò tái chanh.* They disappeared again but shortly returned, this time to a room calmed of ricocheting youngsters now squirming in their seats at their reserved table. I watched Kim patiently help the kids prepare their plates.

Lily placed a dish of honey-braised chicken over vermicelli noodles in front of me and upon her place mat next to mine. Anh followed with spring rolls and brought my chopsticks. Lily scooted in next to me and glanced at my chicken. "You like, GI?" she quipped.

"I do," I said, as Louie Armstrong's "What a Wonderful World" drifted in from the stereo only to suck me into a shameful eddy....I'd warned Lily that who I love gets hurt. But I let her dismiss that threat to invite me. Now I sat here comforted by her while Margo bled.

I forced my light chatter with Lily until I could get her alone to tell her what I did to Margo last night could happen to her. Give her another chance to save herself.

After hardly enjoying the sweet corn pudding that topped off our meals, I joined the adults in clearing the tables. I met Lily at the kitchen sink and told her I needed to tell her something.

Lily turned to her mother and spoke in Vietnamese. Then turned to me, put her arm through mine, and said, "Come." She led me outside to the bench under the oak tree.

As we sat, before I could raise my warning, she said, "You sleep alone last night, didn't you."

Left with a shallow breath, I said, "You—you don't sound surprised."

"You would not be here if you didn't." She tapped my knee once but didn't rest her hand there. "What happen last night?"

Glancing between my loafers and her tennies, I steeled for the truth I'd withheld from Margo and myself. Then told her, "She kicked me out of her bed—I called her Lily."

"Oh." She brought her hand to her mouth and let it drift to her lap. "You said my name in middle of—"

"No! Just before." I puckered in a breath. "She said it stopped me from making love to the wrong woman."

Lily eased her hand upon my thigh and fanned her fingers. "What do you think?"

I felt the sheltering warmth of her touch and gazed upon her fingers. "I didn't realize she was right until I got here."

"You did not know until almost too late."

I looked up, but she turned away in afterthought. She'd caught how grievously I'd fooled myself.

She curled her fingers into a loose fist above my knee. "I cannot make the same mistake."

I braced for rejection.

She turned to me, her eyes surveying my face. "Les, do you know what I do in my spa?"

"Wha—what?" I said fingers splayed, shoulders pinched.

"What do you think I do at my business?"

"You told me—greet customers is all."

Squinting, she shook her head. "Most of the time. But when not enough girls, I must do for customers what Kim do for you."

Instead of axing me, she'd declared *her* deal-breaker. A jealous stab felled my tongue as her fingertips pressed into my thigh. "I open my own place, so I don't have to *all* the time."

"Then don't!" burst out of my mouth.

She let go of my leg as her stare heated into a glare. Her once lyrical tongue spewed staccato. "You are a man. You come and go from my place—nobody judge you. But everybody treat me like a whore since rape. At my spa, I make men pay for what they take."

Startled, I blinked but grasped that she'd forged her outrage into more than a living. Exacting retribution left no tenderness for any man's say. Then, socked by an appalling chill, I strained, "Do you see the man who attacked you when you look at me?"

I watched Lily's eyes cool as her chest heaved in a breath. "You would not be here if I did. But no one respects a man who loves a whore." Lily stood, folded her arms, and looked down at me. "You are a CPA. I can have pride in you. But, you will lose respect with me. If you must go, I understand."

She'd pressed that her scorn would become mine, with no promise to stop fucking strangers....But that she'd given me a lucid choice dulled my covetous spike. "Your job shouldn't matter to me."

Lily rubbed her shoulders. "Not what others think."

Her exposure to *my* secrets not only hadn't injured her but had led to her forgiveness. But the price of her redemption included accepting that her body could be bought by other men. I rose to my feet and looked about her yard as if to see where I stood. Faced with forsaking us both or trusting that the sterile limits of trading sex for money threatened nothing but my jaundiced pride, I spread my arms. "I can't care what others think and lose you. I'll beat my jealousy before I let it get between us."

Lily cupped my shoulders. "I can promise that you will only be the second man I let sleep with me without a condom." Then she stretched up on her tiptoes and gracefully stroked her inhaling nose across my cheek, leaving me aglow in her wake.

A gaggle of pint-sized goofballs popped out her front door, led by Annie in a laughter-stoked catch-me-if-you-can.

We stepped apart. Soon surrounded by bobbing heads, their desperate fingers turned Lily's dress and my pant legs into flagging taunts between predator and prey.

Lily put her hands on her hips. "Maybe we go find another place to talk?"

"Where to?" I said, over squeals of laughter.

"Your apartment?" She reached for my hand as the goofballs spun off toward the trees. "Let's go in, say goodbye, and get my overnight bag."

Surprised, I repeated, "'Overnight bag?'"

Lily placed her warm palm upon my heart. "Don't worry, no charge."

"That's not what I meant."

She patted my chest. "Better not."

Epilogue

DJ scolded me for depriving him of his picture of the princess and the penguin. Cisco called me a *pendejo* for blowing it with Margo. And, their shock that Lily was a madam was annoyingly short-lived. But after I'd told them about Annie, I felt their sincerity as both said they'd look forward to meeting her and her mom.

I'd made no secret to Lily of my grief over burning my best friend of nearly twenty years. When she found out that Margo'd kicked me out of her bed but not her apartment, she'd recognized that Margo'd given me a chance to save the romance. Lily'd said *She love you a lot,* adding that maybe Margo'd let us be friends again since she hadn't spent her body on a lie.

Awkward, I'd asked if she'd be okay with that? *You called her my name. Not me her name,* she'd said in her precise grit.

Despite Lily's support for Margo's friendship, it took mettle to push past my guilt and repeatedly punch in Margo's phone numbers. I'd silently rehearse my scripted amends before each attempt. But months passed without her answering my messages or pages.

It took the Loma Prieta quake to fracture the wall between Margo and me. But navigating through the rubble of a city on fire without power or phones exacted excruciating hours to get to Margo's after ensuring Lily and Annie were home safe.

Long after midnight, I pounded on the door of Margo's thankfully intact condo.

"Who's there?"

"Me, Les," I answered in faint contrast to my desperate pounding.

Margo opened her door, wearing her favorite jeans and bulky sweater. She flung her arms around my neck. "You're alright!"

"The best now," I said, lacing my arms about her waist.

My scripted amends evaporated in her embrace, so it took me a moment to feel that Margo's hands had shifted to my shoulders and gently pushed me away. I dropped my arms.

She stepped back and cleared her throat. "Now I know."

I cocked my head like a puzzled mutt. "What?"

She crossed her arms and squeezed her shoulders. "That I'm more relieved than pissed to see you alive. Come in."

"Thanks?" I said as I followed her into her living room, lit by the same candles blown out on our last night together. Then I saw my jeans and shirt folded against the arm of her couch, topped by my overnight bag. Sitting down from my things stirred my belly. Did she know I'd show up?

Margo took the chair across from me. On the coffee table sat my torn note, anchored by her portable radio droning casualty and damage updates. She turned it off.

"Now that you're here, I can stop arguing with myself about barging in on you and Lily to return your things." She glanced at them and pinched a wounded grin. "And to see that you're okay."

Squeezing my knees, I scattered my gaze between my hands. "She keeps her own home. Has a yard for her little girl, Annie." I looked up to see Margo go stiff, rod rigid, pupils predator keen.

"No match against Lily's beauty *and* Linh Mai's replacement, am I?" Margo thrust her palms up. "Sorry—lost my temper. But I've never been so wounded or angry."

Her hands dropped, and she sheepishly glanced between us. "You know, I called you the morning you left. But once it rang, I knew I only wanted you back. That I was vulnerable to your denial. So I hung up."

Rubbing my thighs, I said, "I'd lied to you and myself about Lily."

Margo leaned forward and slipped my ragged note from under her radio. Her eyes welled as she focused on it. "This bleary plea to fix *what we had* reeked of your denial about Lily, just as her whispered name declared that you'd crawled into bed with the wrong person."

She laid the note on the table, wiped her tears, and cleared her throat. "I've ignored your calls since. Both to avoid hearing the truth about Lily and, I'm ashamed to say, to punish you, too."

I couldn't raise my voice to say I deserved more.

Margo puckered her brow and fell back. "Does Lily know you're here?"

"Ye—yes. She encouraged it."

"You can talk to her about me?" she asked, her voice breathless.

She watched my shaky nod then massaged her collar. "I spoke to my brother about what happened. Bobby always liked you. But when I told him you called me another woman's name, I had to talk him out of kicking your *culo*." Then Margo snickered, "But I didn't stop him from trash-talking you."

"I deserve an ass-kicking."

Margo's eyes drifted away, then back again. "But when Bobby found out that Lily is Vietnamese. You know what he told me?"

Without a clue, I shook my head.

"He said that if his wife Lydia was Vietnamese, he wouldn't have to pull any punches about what he went through because she'd been through it, too. That he could talk to her like he can to other vets." After an ironic chuckle, she added, "I guess his group therapy paid off."

Margo slouched in her seat and looked away. "Made me face how painful it was for me to listen to Linh Mai's horrible loss." She lifted her eyes to mine again. "Is it easier to talk to Lily than me about your little girl?"

"*Easy* isn't the word I'd use, but yes, is the short answer."

Margo stretched back and dug her fingers into the front pocket of her jeans as she blinked about her flickering candles.

She fished out her key to my apartment and pushed it across the table toward me. "Take this to Lily, where it belongs." Then she pulled out the key ring I'd given her. Thumbing the leather braid's turquoise pendant, she asked, "Can I keep this?"

"I'd like you to."

She tucked it back into her pocket and then lifted out the one she'd given me, keyless. She dangled its leather laces between us. "Want this back?"

"I do," I said and reached across the table.

She draped it across my palm. "If Lily lets you keep it, maybe we'll all be friends—someday."

I closed my fingers around the soft strands. "'Someday?'"

"Don't push it, Les."

About the Author

Gregory Montoya is a member of Benicia Literary Arts. His short-short story "The Coat" appeared in the journal *Up Dare?* in 2003, and he self published his mystery novel, *The Powder Room* in 2017. *Madams Wear Black* is born out of his experiences as a U.S. Army Vietnam Era veteran and Veterans Administration Licensed Clinical Social Worker (LCSW), responsible for treating psychological trauma. Being born and raised in California's rich cultural mix has prepared him to distill his characters' journeys through a rich blend of family, friends, and lovers.

Stay tuned for an excerpt from Montoya's first book, "The Powder Room"…

Chapter 1 — THE BLAST

I heard hinges creak behind the bar. My light didn't spot a thing.

"SFPD! Show yourself!" I shouted, whipping out my piece.

"Chief Ferrus. That you, Faeth?" the chief said. His helmet surfaced like a sub from behind the bar. Two more firefighters followed.

"What the hell?" I holstered my SIG.

"Trap door to the basement. Whole block's connected by underground corridors." Ferrus tilted his helmet back with his thumb. "But we kept the fire contained to Bambi's. Gas leak blew."

"Why call Homicide over a gas leak?"

The fire crew had swamped Bambi's Lounge. I bent down to roll up my trousers to keep 'em outta the muck.

He pointed with his chin toward the hall. "Everybody heard the alarm and got out before the blast —everybody except the victim in the ladies' room. And she's holding a gun."

I dropped my cuffs. "Gun, huh? I spoke to the barflies outside. None of 'em smelled smoke or gas till after the explosion. So what tripped the alarm? And what kept the vic inside?"

"Asked myself the same things. That's why I called. By the way, I spotted the edge of a cell phone under your victim's thigh. Don't want ya to miss it."

"You shoulda been a cop, Ferrus."

"Faint at the sight of blood."

"Takes more than a bleed to rattle old-timers like us," I said, shaking my head.

"Who you callin' an old-timer? Say, where's Barbara Jean?"

Proper old Ferrus could never bring himself to call Detective Reeves by her initials: BJ.

"Late as usual. Takes her time tartin' up."

"She's one tall looker."

"About six feet of stacked brick," I said.

"We'll be checking the neighboring buildings if ya need us," Ferrus said.

I nodded and glanced at my watch—one o'clock.

"Dammit," I said out loud. Did I forget to top off Al's cat dish? Hell, fur pig won't starve before I get home, I told myself. Then I lit the scorched hallway in the back toward the powder room and the body.

At the shattered restroom door, I gagged on the stench. Flashes of smoldering bodies burst across my brain. My feet froze.

"Smells like barbecue, don't it, Lo?"

I heard BJ's Texas twang as she barged in the front door.

"Got a victim in there. Point for me." She'd called the presence of a body. Wadded up the vic into a score in our contest for clues.

I flinched, but her icy crack yanked me back to North Beach from Nam. No detective other than BJ got away with calling me Lo. I put my light on her.

"Yeah, I told you when I called that Ferrus found a body in the powder room. Shouldn't count. And show a little respect for the dead."

"But I declared it, didn't I?" she said, combing her thick black bangs with her manicured nails. "One to nothin'." BJ stuffed her nose with cotton.

I lit the former Texas Ranger's way with my flashlight. Her leather jacket ended at the waist of her tight gray slacks. She wore short black boots, and a 35 mm Leica hung from her shoulder just below a wide red belt. Ricky, my gay half brother, would've liked her outfit, I thought, sorry I'd chased him away.

"Don't know why you doll up to dig around a potential murder scene."

"Respect for the dead," BJ quipped.

I snorted, then packed my nose with tissue before turning back to the door. No use bitching about her cold-blooded jibes. I did once, but she'd put me in my place. Said a woman's tears translate as weakness in the world of homicide investigations, adding that if she had testes, chinks in her armor would add up to sensitive. Yeah. She'd made her point.

BJ stepped next to me in the queen-sized restroom, turned her head toward me, and sniffed my cheek. "You been drinkin'?"

I jerked back. "Shot of tequila. Couldn't sleep." The fifteen years since Ricky disappeared had balled up into nightmares about what had happened to him. He'd left in 1994 because I couldn't accept that he was gay. By the time I'd wised up enough not to care, his trail had gone cold.

"Again? You'd sleep better if you had yourself a little company once in a while." BJ knocked her shoulder into mine. "Know what I mean, Lo?"

"That's Detective Faeth to you," I said, but now she'd sloshed up Madge's face. I'd married her a couple of years after Ricky disappeared. Five years later she'd left this graying, balding grump. I couldn't blame her. She'd gotten fed up with me off at the job all the time. And she'd found out I had a brother. Looked straight into my tired brown eyes and griped at me to find Ricky. I shoulda' listened.

"I could call you Detective Lawrence Oliver Faeth. But Lo's faster." BJ covered her mouth in a fake attempt to stop a giggle.

I poked my light into her hazel eyes and stole a line from Robin Williams: "If you weren't a girl, I'd rip your lips off and paste them to your eyes so you could watch what you say."

"Go on, take your best shot, dahlin'. But you ought to let Lupe fix you up. Or do you still have the hots for her, feeling safe from those fires 'cause she's married to your amigo?"

My face tingled. I should have never taken her to Frank and Lupe's place, Mac's Bar and Grill. The closest thing I could call a hangout. BJ'd noticed my temperature rise in front of Lupe.

"Fix me up? I wouldn't waste anybody's time. And can that 'hots for Lupe' crap. She's my pal's wife, for god's sake."

"Coward. The least a partner can do is pry you outta' your shell." BJ rocked her head in time with her twang.

"Shell?" I growled. "Al's plenty of company and in a pinch, there's Star Trek reruns." My light landed on the charred corpse. "A woman," I said to change the subject. The explosion had twisted her to the floor. I prayed death had been quick.

"Nailed the vic's gender, did ya? What gave it up? The dress or that she's in the little girl's room?"

"Suppose that squares us in your cheap-ass points department," I said over the suck of my heels against the muddy floor.

I focused my light on the corpse's hand and its nickel-plated revolver. "She's got a pistol," I announced for a point ahead, then saw the cell partially covered by her thigh. I slid that bit of information up my points sleeve.

"Pistol?" BJ asked.

"Suspicious, huh?" I said, but BJ stepped back.

"Just because she's in a dress doesn't mean she's a she. This is San Francisco, remember?" Then BJ's voice sank. "Or do shims make Detective Faeth a little squirrelly?"

"Shims?" I said, bracing for another dig. Despite keeping a lid on my revulsion toward homos, she'd seen through me. Needled me every chance she got.

"You know, dahlin'. He-shes. Boys that dress like girls."

"Don't start. I'm not in the mood," I said to block Ricky's drag-queen sashay from my baggy eyes. "Call it a hunch, BJ. This is North Beach. Not the gay Castro. And like you said, she's in a dress and in the ladies' room."

I focused on the course of the blast. Debris had ricocheted off walls, splintered the powder room door, and fractured the roof. A streetlight's scrawny ray poked through the ceiling.

"We've stepped into the center of the blast," BJ said, stealing what I was about to say. She slipped her digital recorder out of her pocket and described the scene.

"Looks like ground zero to me too," I said, unable to better my own conclusion.

BJ coughed into her fist and flicked off the recorder. "All right, Mr. Self-Reliant, ready for me to capture the moment?" She slid the camera from her shoulder. "Still life with cop and corpse."

"Leave me out of it." I stepped out of her way and into a puddle. "Shit." Braced against a buckled stall, I poured ink out of my loafer.

"Smile, Lo." Using her cell phone, she snapped a picture of me draining my shoe.

I flipped her off, but she'd turned to the victim.

"Get a picture of that gun," I said

With each click of the Leica, she got a pic, and I got a flash of her steps around the corpse. The bursts of light left me with afterimages of twisted pipes and shattered toilet bowls. BJ crouched next to the body and picked up the glob that had been the victim's plastic purse. "Found her purse for my point up."

"Hey, get your gloves on, will ya'?" Though the fire had likely melted away any prints, I guessed BJ snubbed protocol to remind me that I didn't intimidate her. I liked that about her.

"Prints wouldn't have survived on this lump," BJ said, waving the purse at me with her naked fingers.

I nodded. "Without prints or ID, Forensics will have to use DNA or dental records to identify the poor gal."

"Pretty sure the 'poor gal' is a she, huh?" BJ plunked the purse into an evidence bag. Stuffed it into her jacket pocket.

I raised my voice. "Oh, that's right. She's alone. She must be a he. Real women hit the head in twos, right?"

She glanced at me twice before looking back at the vic. I'd expected an eye roll. Had my crack hit a nerve?

The "Dixie" jingle of BJ's cell phone interrupted us. As she stood up from the remains, her face glowed in her phone's backlit display.

"Gimme a sec." Without another word, she tiptoed around the rubble and disappeared into the hall.

I'd never seen her take a private call. "What the hell, BJ? It's almost two in the morning. Somebody fix you up?" I barked after her.

Silence.

* * *

"Hell's bells, there's no sign of Rosie," BJ whispered into her phone to Dr. Marilee Crusher, grande dame of the secret women's order, Once-a-Dick-Always-a-Dick or what members affectionately called O'DAD. She slogged farther away from the ladies' room. Rosie-the-Riveter posters identified powder rooms with O'DAD's exclusive Wi-Fi hot spots. The thought of the sisterhood hijacking the World War II icon usually tickled her. But not tonight.

"Rosie musta been destroyed by the fire," she said. The hot spot, plus the vic's gun, knocked the body in the powder room from the column of accident victim into the latest tally of her target's prey.

"You didn't know. Have you called in the CSI team?"

BJ caught a hint of dread in Marilee's tone. Mild compared to her own.

"Not yet. Being busy and dumb luck is all that's stopped me from calling 'em in." BJ strained to steady her voice, gripped by her failure to stop the murders.

She pushed her fingers through her hair. Her eyes darted about the blackened lounge but registered nothing. If news of the killings got out, O'DAD, the FBI's off-the-grid asset in the war on terror, risked exposure.

"At least we'll avoid them. The three of us will come in through the basement to remove the cable and retrieve our hardware as soon as the fire department leaves. Your partner must be gone before we arrive. Otherwise…well, you know." Marilee's voice slid into a sigh.

BJ understood Marilee's sag. If she couldn't extricate Lo before they arrived, his sanity would be trounced by an O'DAD gaslight scheme. A sacrifice she and Marilee wished to avoid. But it was Marilee's "three of us" that frosted her. She knew that included the killer and her enforcer.

"Gettin' Detective Faeth outta here will be like prying a hen off her eggs." She heard her voice climb and peered over her shoulder for signs of Lo. All that followed her was an ashen breeze.

"Are your loyalties confused?"

"I can't believe you asked me that." Her reply sharpened by her envy of Marilee's bond with the other orphan, the killer. BJ had discovered that Marilee and her target's mother were like sisters. Mom killed herself in 1982. More than once, BJ had endured Marilee's dismissing her surrogate daughter's homicidal bitterness as harmless. And now Marilee had the gall to question her.

BJ pounded her hip.

"I apologize. I'm upset," Marilee said. "A gas explosion just took a life, and now it threatens to expose us. On top of that, unless you remove your partner before we arrive, we'll have to destroy his credibility. I couldn't blame you if you're conflicted."

"I don't care that it's Faeth. But neither one of us likes turning anybody into O'DAD's rodeo clown," BJ said to deflect her grief

"Do what you can to remove him before we arrive, hon. You've got until the firefighters leave. Then we have to come in."

"Will do." BJ spoke crisply and then tapped off her O'DAD cell. She had little time to bounce Lo out of Bambi's. She considered faking fatigue. Maybe she'd nitpick to ignite his combustible impatience. She could stop challenging him to wrap up sooner than later.

After taking in a sooty breath, she exhaled through her nose. Such improvised efforts would be out of character and not be missed by the wily Lo. But BJ knew that Lo's contact with Marilee's team would force her to ignite a gaslight against him. And if the killer decided the old hound caught O'DAD's scent, it would be his life that was at risk.

She tromped back toward the powder room.

Other Titles from Last Laugh Productions

The Nearest Place Distant, by Stephen Francis Cosgrove

Hint, by Deborah L. Fruchey

Shattered Windows, by Deborah L. Fruchey

Eye Masks, by Rudy Jon Tanner

What Still Matters, by Johanna Ely

We'll Always Have Stockton, by Steve Arntson

The Worlds According to Loki, 2nd Edition, by Vampyre Mike Kassel

For Whoever Thinks a Piano is Furniture, by Rudy Jon Tanner

The Hall of Painted Sonnets, Sonnets by Steve Arntson, Art by Diane Lee Moomey

Embodied (hardcover), by Jan Dederick

Gypsy & Other Poems, by Steve Arntson

Armageddon Bootcamp…and other poems (hardcover), by Maria Elizabeth Rosales

Three Kinds of Dark (ebook, hardcover), by Deborah L. Fruchey

Touchstones (hardcover), by Maria Elizabeth Rosales

Priestess of Secrets, by Deborah L. Fruchey

Bat Flower: poems, plays & other perversions, by Vampyre Mike Kassel

Armadillo (ebook, hardcover), by Deborah L. Fruchey

Color Cards & Self Healing, by Jean Luo

The Colors of Sound (companion CD or MP3), performed &
composed by Robert Hamaker

A Scandalous Creature, by Deborah L. Fruchey

Mental Illness Ain't for Sissies, by Deborah L. Fruchey

The Unwilling Heiress, by Deborah L. Fruchey

Island Journey (Instrumental CD or MP3), composed &
performed by Robert M. Hamaker

Island Journey (Narrated Meditation CD or MP3), by Robert M.
Hamaker, narrated by Deborah Fruchey

Crystal Connections (CD or MP3), by Robert M. Hamaker & Erik
Satie *(gymnopodie #1)*

Crystalline Sleep (Binaural Beats CD or MP3), by Robert M.
Hamaker